KEY WEST CURSE

A Jack Marsh Thriller

Mike Pettit

Key West Curse

Mike Pettit

©copyright 2017 Key West Curse, Mike Pettit

Dedication

First Sergeant Robert L. Pettit, U.S.M.C.

R.I.P.

Key West Curse

Chapter 1

The *Sea Bird Explorer*, with her crew of six, sat upon the calm waters of the Caribbean Sea, barely rocking as the men in the wheelhouse bent over the charts and silently studied them for the tenth time. The *ping* from the sonar hitting the wreck three hundred feet under the keel of the deep-water salvage ship was not what had the team perplexed. The initial ping was off the rusted hull of an obsolete Soviet diesel submarine belonging to the Cuban Navy. The odd secondary return is what had the men baffled. The ghost pings were like echoes trailing the initial ping at three-minute intervals. If one compared the sonar ping to a church bell clapper striking the bell, then the secondary ping would be the sound of a bell in the next town over, distinct, but distant.

Austin Burke had been in the salvage business for forty years and had never experienced this delayed bounce-back before. He was an expert and had found wrecks all over the world. He had become known as an authority on deep sea salvage; if there was a wreck around, Burke would find it. This particular exploration was on his and a few investors backs. For years, the area in the very center of the Caribbean Sea had fascinated him and had called to him like sirens on a distant shoal. The lure wasn't a whimsical urge, but a salvager's curiosity at the odd strata of the ocean bed that rose from over nine thousand feet to just under three hundred feet below the water's surface. His boat, the *Sea Bird*

Explorer, sat right atop the apex of what he and his crew had been surveying for the last two weeks. If all the satellite charts were correct, the underwater mount ran east of the Nicaragua bank, south of the Jamaican Trough, and north of the Columbian basin and its thirteen thousand foot depths. The mount fell off at a fifteen-degree angle towards Jamaica for about fifty kilometers before it flattened out on the seabed in seven thousand feet of water. Off to the west, the mount ended abruptly, dropping from a gentle slope of six thousand feet to a seventy-degree angle, bottoming out at nine thousand feet. The entire shape resembled a teardrop with the bulk of the drop along the southern lip pointing towards Columbia and Venezuela, and the tail tapering off towards Jamaica.

"It just ain't possible, Austin," Dick Chandler said as he listened intently to returning echoes on his headphones. "There's got to be a scientific explanation to what we're hearing."

"Yeah, I agree Dick. But my numbers and calculations keep coming up with the same answer. We need to get down there and take a look, maybe tap a small hole through the hull to see what we have," Austin said, stepping back from the chart table and wiping his eyes in frustration.

"That means we'll have to leave the area so we can get a few deep divers and more lift equipment out here, unless you plan to use the submersible to sniff around. I mean we could do it. It shouldn't take more than a few passes with

Petuna down there. Let her sniff around and taste what we got."

Petuna was an expensive computerized seabed explorer which imitated the five senses of the human body and had initially been developed by NASA for the Mars probe. The probe had been redesigned and customized by Burke's engineers to do just about everything the Mars unit could do. It was housed to resemble an octopus with all the computerization in a cylinder about six feet long, with probe like tentacle-legs that stuck out from around one end of the cylinder that grasped the ocean floor and stabilized the cylinder in an upright position. The cylinder used a combination of lasers, sonar impulses, and optical energy to penetrate solids several miles thick, sending back signals of everything it tasted, smelled, saw, and felt. It could routinely tell the difference between sand and water, iron and gold, basalt and quartz. The chemical makeup of any substance could be analyzed and returned in moments.

Austin Burke knew the only thing more valuable aboard ship was Sophie, his big golden retriever. When the divorce from his wife of thirty years came through, his lawyer thought he was insane for wanting the dog and nothing more. His wish came true. Now he had his dog, his boat— the *Sea Bird Explorer*— and several large loans from investors in this gamble in the middle of the Caribbean Sea. If this exploration didn't pan out with something, he figured he would go down to Brazil and hire out on a shrimper.

"It's too late in the day to launch *Petuna*. Let's shut everything down and take a break. We all need some downtime," Austin said. "Let's throw a few lines over the side and catch us some dinner."

"Better yet, let's go over the side and choose dinner," Dick said, with a big grin on his face as he headed for the scuba-gear locker.

—

Late the next day, the two men were sitting surprised by their findings, the four other crew members were battening down the *Sea Bird* in preparation for heading home. *Petuna* had done her job well, the data was in, and the analysis completed. Austin Burke and his team had discovered the Cuban submarine El President Fidel Castro. At the time the sub sank it was reported to contain over five billion dollars in gold bars taken from the Venezuelan treasury. Knowing that he was dying, Hugo Chavez ordered that the gold be transferred to Havana for safe keeping while his unpopular socialist government transitioned after his death. His successor was to be Nicolás Maduro, his confidante and fellow socialist. Chavez knew the people despised Maduro and wanted to make sure that if Maduro was toppled the country's wealth would disappear with him. Within hours of Chavez dying, the Minister of the Treasury announced that the gold bullion was missing and that a full scale investigation had been ordered by President Maduro. After a flurry of news releases and feelers going out through

Interpol the episode died down and nothing more was ever said about the missing bullion, until now.

The gold wasn't what had confounded the too old salvagers. If Petuna's readouts were correct, there was something sealed in a two-thousand-pound lead container in the forward compartment of the sub.

"What the hell could it be! What was Chavez hiding inside a block of lead? Are we talking some kind of bomb, some nuclear device. Is it already weapon's grade fissional material?" Dick said.

"If it is weapons grade this would be more than enough to wipe out Galveston or Port Arthur."

"Never happen Austin. Venezuela, nor Cuba have a delivery system. Fat chance they could pull it off."

"You're not thinking, old boy. Think one man with a duffle bag, that's all it would take. Blow a hole in Midtown Manhattan during rush hour and you got yourself fifty thousand dead and hundreds of thousands more burned and injured."

"My God. Is it even possible! Thousands of square miles of sea and we found it tucked in a crevice like a damned hotdog in a bun. No wonder no one ever found it. Unless you were right on top of it, the sonar would never pick it up," Dick said.

"Yeah, we found it all right, now what do we do about it. The biggest find of my life and what happens, a bomb's strapped to it…."

"Not really, in its current state it isn't dangerous at all. We just bring the gold up and let Mother Nature keep the lead case."

Austin looked at his friend, and shook his head. "The bomb I'm talking about is the attention this is going to bring. We'll have every Navy ship in the Caribbean on top of us the second word gets out."

"This is bigger than the Glomar Explorer, the Cortez treasure ship, Goring's U-Boat… all put together. Think of it, five billion in gold bars in our back yard, and it's ours. Damn Austin, we're rich, forget about what may or may not be inside the lead case. We just keep our yaps shut and bring the bullion up" Dick said jubilantly, grabbing Austin's arm and starting to do a square dance.

"Ok, that's enough," Austin said, laughing. "We ain't rich yet. There are a million things that have to be done before the first cable drops over the side, like keeping this secret while we pull everything together that we'll need to pull it up."

"No sweat, Austin. We just go to the Navy and sit back and collect on shares."

"Naw, this is too big. This is going to be big trouble if we don't do it right. This is a game-changer. Think about it, every sonofabitch in the Caribbean will want to claim it. Most of them are Chavez's buddies, too. You can bet Fidel and that thief brother of his, Raul, will be all over this. Not to mention Maduro, too. Venezuela's pogroms have come to a screaming halt...no dinero, no pogroms. Now they're just shooting anyone they please. No, Dick, we need to be smart about this. I don't want us to be scared, but something like this could get us killed very quick-like if we go off halfcocked."

"Yeah, I hear ya. Hell, even the enviro-whackos would be on our ass, plus our own government with those pantywaists in Washington pushing their 'share the wealth' B.S."

"Dick, you're the one with the contacts. You know a hell of a lot more people than I do in the government, many more than me when it comes to knowing who to talk to. All I know is that if we shoot off our mouths about the lead case before we have checked and double-checked everything, we'll be in the hurt locker for sure."

"Cap'n Austin, we're battened down and ready to go when you are," Tiny Miles, the *Sea Bird's* skipper said.

"Let's make for Kingston, Tiny. Give me an ETA once you've got your GPS, plotted. I'll need the sat-phone also. I've got to make a call to the mainland as soon as we're up."

CHAPTER 2

The big red rooster swung upside down from a hemp rope hanging from a rafter. Its feet were tightly tied just above the animal's spurs that slashed and fought the binding. The wings were spread in a full feathered fan, beating the air uselessly, as the eyes blinked, focused, blinked, focused again as the head made jerking movements in terror. Shadows bounced off the wood-slat walls and sparse furnishings. Shelves held glass jars and bowls of herbs and poultices made from centuries-old recipes. Cheap candles burned around the room with their weak light hiding more in shadows than their waxy rays revealed. The smell of burning feathers mixed with dung and ganja weed lay heavy in the air.

Two women sat in a corner, beating rhythmically on leather skins stretched taught across open-ended tin cans. Their eyes were watery, wide in a trance-like spell as their Priestess swayed nude over the body of a white man stretched prone on a mattress of animal skins and fresh cut branches from the gumbo-limbo trees.

The old Priestess was less than five feet in height, although she was well into her eighties or nineties. At this moment, she appeared to her acolytes as having transformed into a young and well-endowed virgin with large shapely breasts and beautifully formed buttocks. Her skin was the blackest of black, her hair stood out in clumps of seemingly electrified tangles that undulated like snakes as she chanted in an ancient African language spoken only by a few who had been blessed by the ancient gods back in the beginning when giants roamed the earth.

The woman called herself Mama Dey around Key West, a tropical haven that sits at the end of the line for those on the run. She walked the streets selling flowers and packs of gum to tourists from an old woven basket along with the occasional quick palm reading. The locals all knew that Mama had the *Shine,* and her predictions were usually right on the money. Rich and poor alike would consult her on business ventures, conception, naming a newborn, and money matters. Then there were the ones who paid her for her secret powers to cast out demons, hurt someone, cause a sickness…the darker side of the *Shine.* No one knew for sure where she came from, or when she had arrived. Her age was believed to be in the eighties, but there are old stories of her, or someone very similar to her, around Key West helping the locals during the huge devastating hurricane of 1872 that took every third resident and left only the turtle kraals standing. She would disappear occasionally for weeks and months at a time. One day she was there, the next gone. Her small cottage, located deep in Old Town, was taboo, and no one ever entered without her permission, no matter what they heard, or thought they saw behind the feed-sack curtained windows.

Tonight Mama Dey was fighting a powerful spirit. She had tried to reason with it at first, but it struck out at her with a barbed tail. She quickly splattered urine from a cup on it, and it went away only to return as a helpless chimp asking for food. She knew food was a ploy used by this particular spirit, Baba Dey, to throw her off her prayers. Baba would steal a man's soul, if he were not alert and on guard to fight it. The evil spirit especially attacked men who had given up on life, or had suffered the loss of self-image, or thought themselves unworthy for whatever reasons. Drunkards, or men with no religious belief. or guilt, were prime targets for Baba. This man lying on her cottage floor was such a man. By all reports, he should be strong and healthy, a man among men. It was reported that he had killed many men, and that powerful men feared and respected him. But the spirit of Baba owned him and held him tightly to his scaly chest, slowly destroying him, sucking the strength out of him. Mama knew how to win this particular battle, and she redoubled her efforts. She poured a thick syrupy stream from a gourd into the man's mouth and held his nose while he gagged it down. She massaged a gooey salve made from root worms and small beetles mixed in goat waste over his stomach and intestines, then finished him off with a huge lungful of ganja, blown up his nostrils while she held his mouth closed.

"Shuka Imbala, Mkaka Tusta! I command you! Pull the black worm out this man! Baba Dey hiding inside! eating this man! He no match for you, Shuka Tusta! I command you to eat Baba Dey! Shit him out! Kill him! I command you!" Mama screamed out, her whole body shaking, her arms flapping bird-like. Her shadow reflected off the room's walls, magnified out of proportion, resembling primeval spirit dancers in an ancient cave.

The rooster's head suddenly exploded in a shower of blood, splattering over the man and the priestess. Mama's eyes rolled back in her head, her body was trembling and shaking. Urine ran down her legs and splattered the floor. Tears, mixed with mucus from her nose, splotched her cheeks and upper lip. The drumbeaters' hands were a blur as their heads seemingly rolled around on their axis, tongues lolling out, bleating like goats. The room became filled with smoke and stench from the rooster's smoldering feathers as it jittered around on its tether. The man's chest heaved, and black bile shot out of his mouth, spattering the naked woman who was dancing over him. Mama suddenly started crowing like a rooster, her body jerking in all directions at once. The man's bowels suddenly exploded and a black watery mess shot out of his rectum. A loud roar came out of the mouth of the Priestess, and she collapsed onto the floor, unconscious. The drummers lay slumped over their instruments, the rooster swung dead on its pendulum, the man was unmoving, but breathing deeply after going through the traumatic event.

Soft wind coming off the ocean cleared the room of the ganja's burnt-offering and stench. The occupants of the cottage slept deeply. Outside, several locals blessed and crossed themselves against whatever had occurred in the old cottage, holding amulets and the odd crucifix with the Black Christ to ward off any spirits that may have escaped the clutches of Mama Dey. Ancient Spirits were out in the trees tonight; you could feel them swooping around as you hurried home to safety. Soon, the night lay silent around the narrow streets of Old Town.

Jack Marsh couldn't remember much that occurred over the next few days, other than Mama Dey spoon-feeding him some kind of grits with an awful taste to it. She said it was to heal his gut where that *Devil* yanked everything around inside him. At some point, Max and Chief showed up and carefully loaded him in Max's Island Taxi for the five-block ride home. Once they had him in bed all propped up with pillows, and cold juice in a carafe on the nightstand, they took their leave.

The little bungalow had been cleaned from top to bottom, smelling fresh, like a tropical flower shop. He felt good for the first time in months. He couldn't explain exactly how he felt, other than clear-headed and pain-free. The last couple of years, he had been through one death-defying escapade after another, and the last three months had been spent in an alcohol-induced stupor that took him to the edge of sanity. Now, through some kind of hocus-pocus poultices and secret-sauces, he felt like a new man. He was still weak from the lack of nutrition and abuse to his system, but he was on the road back.

His physical recovery was going to be a piece of cake compared to the healing he would have to go through making amends to all those that he hurt over the last few months. He shuddered at the memory of trashing the Sand Bar in an alcoholic craze, breaking tables and chairs, throwing a bottle of booze and breaking the mirror behind the bar. When Coco Duvalier tried to stop him, he slapped her, knocking her to the ground. He accused Lamont of stealing from the tip jar and fired him, telling him to never return or he would see that he was sent back to prison for violating his parole. When Chief arrived to help get Jack under control, Jack fought him to the ground and told him he was beached and to never go on the *Island Girl* again. Chief took him at his word and moved his gear off the next day. The *Island Girl* had been tied dockside ever since, algae and seaweed covering her once-pristine hull.

Now, Jack was crying at the vague memory of that night. The thought of having hit Coco made him physically ill. When Chief and Max Simms arrived at Mama Dey's to bring him home, he was overwhelmed with self-loathing and love for both of those men. Even though he had treated them horribly, they came back when he needed them most. There is no value a man can place on true friendship and love. It is priceless.

He shook out one of Mama Dey's homemade hand-rolled pills from the jelly-jar she had placed them in and washed it down with a glass of pineapple juice. He called them dung balls. He had no idea what they were made of, but Mama said, "*Take them, or that Devil, he come back*!" He was asleep in less than a minute.

The black boney finger probed deep into the fleshy abdomen, poking around the liver and stomach, then jerked back, and repeated the process again, but more gently.

"Jack, I tink your gut she betta," Mama Dey said. "It be two weeks since dat devil run off. My spirit, she says your body no more sick. Even your mind normal thinking again. You say Mama Dey magic no work. Ha! She work on white mon, black mon, all the same, devil be devil. Dat all there be to dat."

He hated to agree with her, but she was right. He hadn't felt this good in months. His hands were steady, the craving for booze was gone, and his appetite was coming back. His binge drinking after Briar Malone left quickly turned into a constant blackout state from the alcohol. He stayed drunk for more than three months, and only had snapshots of all the crazy things he had done during that time. He turned the Sand Bar over to Coco after having wrecked the place in a drunken rage. The worse thing he did though was to strike Coco, his closest friend. He despised himself for that. He moved out of the apartment over the bar and bought this small house in one of the back alleys so he could drink without being around people. When Briar left, his world flipped over. He had never felt so deeply in love before. Even though they swore they would remain friends forever, he knew she was gone out of his life for good. He used that as his excuse for drinking himself into oblivion. Deep inside he knew that Briar wasn't the only reason. He was deeply troubled inside over his life and had made booze his escape.

The residents of Key West, even as eclectic as they are, gossiped about some of the things he had done. Duval, the main drag, had seen it all. He cringed and thought his antics would just become part of the lore about all the other losers and lost souls who end up in the Keys. Every now and then a quick flash of memory would jolt his system with a spurt of adrenaline. Remorse? No, just anger at himself for sinking into the abyss of alcoholism.

"Mama, I don't know what all you did to me, but I feel great. I'm thinking that maybe I'm ready to start exercising and jogging again. Maybe even think about going back to work."

"Never mind dat. There be plenty time to work. You just eat what I tell you, and you be big and strong in no time. Just eat them broths I give you and you be betta by 'n by," Mama Dey said, as she bundled up her basket of poultices and unguents. "Me, I gotta git. A new baby calling Mama Dey dat needs birfing over to Old Town. I swear that Cloris have one more baby I put a curse on her kluklu." She laughed at her own joke as she stood to leave.

At the front door, Mama paused for a moment with her eyes closed tight, her toothless gums working in silence,

"A man coming around, he bringing fire and water, big trouble coming to da Islands. You going to have to swim, Jack," Mama said, as if from a trance. "Dat be all there be to dat." Then she was out the door.

Jack watched her close the gate to his small yard and start down the alley. The alley was overgrown with coconut trees, bougainvillea, lime and orange trees, all loaded with fruit. The smell of a million different tropical flowers filled the air, all hanging over wood fences and abandoned yards making the alley appear like a peaceful tropical trail.

A chill ran up Jack's spine, even though the trade winds were blowing in from the southeast.

'What was she talking about? What man? Water? Fire? Christ!'

He sat in a hammock chair that hung from a beam running across the open ceiling. He bought the place while hammered out of his mind three months ago. The two guys who had sold him the small island house ran the bed and breakfast that sat on the front of the property on Fleming street, a couple of blocks off Duval. One of the guys had a flare for decorating and really did an outstanding job of bringing the *Island* feel to the place.

An outdoor shower off the bedroom was Jack's favorite space. Three bamboo walls gave the room privacy and the water was at a constant eighty-six degrees. The bedroom had a double bed with a mosquito net over it that almost filled the entire space. The kitchen / living room were all one open space, furnished with a cushioned bamboo couch and chair, and a small dining table with two chairs. The front porch had an overhang from the corrugated tin roof and a two-seater swing hanging from a crossbeam. An identical bungalow sat ten feet away. If his place hadn't been painted yellow and the other blue, he probably would have staggered into the wrong house on many a dark night. Actually, that's how he met Claire Marlow.

Claire lived in the bungalow across the yard from him. She was a civilian doctor at the Navy Base and worked shifts. One night, he made his way back from a night of doing the Duval Crawl, and crawled into the wrong bungalow. Claire had been nice about it and helped him back to his cottage. Since then she had adopted him by checking every morning to make sure he was still among the living. She even sat with him through a couple of bouts with the D.T.'s and other times while he raged and wallowed in self-pity. Why she did it, he didn't know. There is nothing worse than being around a self-absorbed drunk who thinks the world is against him. One night, Claire sat with him while he nursed a particularly severe hangover. He wasn't drunk, but he wasn't sober, either. Jack had been in that stage known to AA people as saturation. Usually when you hit that level, there is no return ticket. You continue to drink and die, or you must quit totally and never go back again. Claire told him about a woman she knew who could cure him if he wanted it badly enough. This woman had helped several of her acquaintances to kick drugs, eating disorders, mood problems, you name it, *Mama* could fix you up. Jack had laughed and told her he could quit on his own anytime. He just didn't want to.

The next day he had a grand mal seizure and was in bad shape. Claire and Donny, one of the B&B owners, put him in a cab and took him to Mama's for "treatment." Jack was there for three days, unconscious, unaware of the things being fed into his body, rubbed through its pores, and more importantly, the mystical prayers and chants ministered to his sick mind and soul. When he came to, he was in his bed, in clean pajamas, and awoke without the shakes or nausea. He lay there for a while checking out different parts of his body. He could smell flowers and fresh coffee. His joints didn't hurt; his stomach was not on fire... he determined that he was dead. At that moment, Claire came in with a tray of toast and eggs, along with a huge mug of steaming coffee. Jack couldn't keep his eyes off Claire as he devoured the breakfast. He had never really seen her except through a drunken haze or a shadow in the night sitting by his bed as he fought off the angel of death. She was probably the most beautiful woman he had ever seen... dark brown hair in a short cut, green eyes and heavy brows and lashes, a nice nose, maybe a touch off center, lips that were fascinating to watch as she talked. Nice dimples and a strong chin. He was in love with her from that first morning and couldn't get enough of being around her. He could tell that she felt the same, but for some reason both were shy about saying anything too emotional to each other. So they just kept things simple. What do you like? What's your favorite food? Blah, blah blah. But inside, he wanted to grab her and squeeze her until she popped. He wanted to scream out that he had finally found the one, nothing else mattered. He would stay here forever if she asked. A momentary pang of guilt thumped at his heart as the image of Briar boarding the plane for L.A., waving and throwing a kiss. There would always be a special place for Briar in Jack's heart.

CHAPTER 3

The rain shower had been heavy as it rolled through Key West, leaving everything fresh and clean in its wake. Jack was sitting on his porch listening to rain droplets dripping into little puddles around the yard. Thunder rumbled off to the west as the storm headed for the Dry Tortugas. Little green tree frogs were belting out a pretty good RAP rhythm—probably one of Snoop Dog's— gecko's were feasting on no-see-ums and mosquitoes.

After an hour of sitting around doing nothing, he was bored and went out for a walk. He wanted to stay away from Duval Street where all the bars and wild party people hung out. He missed the Sand Bar but knew he must stay away from it until he had the cravings under control. He thought about going aboard the *Island Girl* for a couple of days, but remembered that Chief had the boat in Mobile getting its hull cleaned and painted. He strolled over to an internet café off William Street. The place wasn't crowded; it never was. He ordered a Café con Leche and took an open computer. A guy with a shaved head brought the coffee over and an electronic key to plug into the unit.

"Haven't seen you around for a few weeks…you doing ok?" the guy said.

"Yeah, I'm fine. I was a little under the weather for a while, but I'm on the road to recovery now. Thanks for asking."

"Hey, we were worried about you. The last time you were in we put you in a pedi-cab at closing time. We didn't know where you lived so we told the cabbie to drop you off at Sloppy Joes."

"Do I owe you any money? Did I break anything?"

"Naw, nothing like that. We just have to take care of each other, you know what I'm saying?"

"Yeah, thanks again," Jack said, and meant it.

CHAPTER 4

Outside of some remote Central American villages, Key West is the only airport that has chickens roaming free inside the terminal and out on the tarmac, pecking away at the dusty coral in search of insects, crumbs, and bugs. Years ago, the City Council had passed a law that allowed chickens to roam free anywhere in the city. A stiff fine was imposed on anyone who tried to harm or kill the birds. The purpose of the chickens hearkened back to earlier times, when the string of Keys running from Key Largo to Key West were just coral and mangrove swamps with billions of mosquitoes thriving in the brackish water, living off the blood off the indigenous animals. When Jack Flagler built his railroad from Miami to Key West, his work crews were ridden with malaria and fevers from the mosquitos. Flagler even had a belfry built on Sugar Loaf Key, and imported thousands of bats in hopes of eradicating the swarms of mosquitoes. Not long after, the bats didn't like the heat and humidity, and flew back up north. Chickens proved to be the answer. Thousands were let go around the railroad construction site and as it worked its way to Key West, the birds followed. At one time, the city adopted the chicken as part of the City Seal until after the turn of the century when the conch became the city's emblem. Since then the residents called themselves Conchs, *rather than chickens,* Jack concluded.

The Cessna 208 Caravan rolled to an area down from the civilian terminal and pumped its brakes, bouncing to a stop. The name on the side of the fuselage read "Island Air Cargo." Jack spotted Tom sitting in the co-pilot's seat and waved to him. Tom and the pilot spent a couple of minutes shutting down the engines and going through the shutdown check-off list. The side door opened and a set of steps folded down, Tom Parker, Jack's closest friend from their days in the Marine Corps, jumped down to the tarmac and quickly placed the chalking blocks.

"Jackie, God dammit! Get over here and give me a squeeze," Tom yelled out as he came around the wings with his arms spread and a big smile on his face.

"Damn it's good to see you, Bro," Jack said as they hugged. "It's been a long time, Tom."

"You look like shit, Jack. Jeez, what'd those towel heads do to you?" Tom asked as he held him at arm's length.

"Not much, nothing I couldn't handle. They were some tough customers, every one of them was ready to die for Allah. The Egyptian guys were the tough ones. When Briar and I found the sarcophagus and the mutts that took it, the Egyptians did a permanent number on them."

"Yeah, well I say we go back there and do some serious hurt to the mothers. You, Chief, and me can kick some butt and be back in time for Monday night's Dolphins game. Whatcha say, Bro?"

"Count me out. I never want to see another muzzy, Tom. Makes my gonads tingle just thinking about it." He joked, but was dead serious. "Come on, let's get out of here. We have a lot of catching up to do."

Max Simms had his taxi cooled down and ready to roll. He greeted Tom with a flourish and a bow.

"Welcome to our humble island, sir. I have heard many war stories about you. Most of them were how Jack saved you from enemy fire."

"Saved me! Don't believe a word of it. As I recall, I was the one doing the saving, and have a nasty bullet hole to show for it.

Max pulled into the alley just as Claire was coming out of the gate in her doctor's scrubs, heading for work at the Navy hospital off Truman Avenue.

"Hi, Jack," she said with a beautiful smile, "who's the clone look-alike?"

"He's no clone; he's my buddy...older buddy, much older. You won't like him, he's a pervert from L.A., he likes goats." Jack said in mock seriousness.

"Step aside and let me speak to this lady," Tom said, as he pushed Jack out of the way. "If you don't know by now, you need to know, that my pal here is a phony and has three wives up on the mainland and nine kids at the last count. You're safer with me than Bozo here," he said with a wink.

"I don't know. I kind of like married men, especially those with three or more. You are cute, though," Claire said coyly.

"OK let's break this up. I don't like the direction this is going," Jack said, as he pushed the two apart at arm's length, "Tom, I was here first. She's mine," he said protectively.

"Really Jack, am I yours?" Claire said with a twinkle in her eyes.

"Well…. yes, I guess," he stuttered like a teenager.

"Well, hold that thought. I'll see you after work tonight. I'm going to be late, again. And Tom, stick around so you can tell me all about his other wives."

"It'll take a couple of days, but I'll tell ya everything, I promise, Scouts honor," Tom said, as Claire unlocked her bike and pedaled off down the alley, waving good-bye.

Later, Tom was chewing on the last slice of pizza and licking his fingers and smacking his lips,

"Now that's a pizza. That was almost as good as the pies we used to get at the NCO club at on Okinawa. There was a Japanese fry cook that learned how to make 'em from an old Italian Gunnery Sergeant. Ah, those were the days! Back when I was a corporal and didn't have a care in the world. Drink a little plum wine, chase the broads out in the 'ville, catch a little field duty. That was the life, Bro." Tom said as he stretched and yawned.

"Yeah, well those days are gone. What you're telling me now is that we may have some *Field Duty* on our hands with this Burke dude."

"Hey Jack, I told you. He's good people. He saved my ass in Fallujah. If it weren't for him, I'd still be there. I owe him. You were a Marine; you know we got to stick together." Tom had made the Marine Corp his career and was a hundred percent gung-ho.

"Tom, I'm out of the Corps. That's all a distant nightmare. I gave them six years, and that was enough. I understand all the esprit de corps crap, the band of brothers' stuff, but this sounds like trouble coming at us. I say we pass."

"Jack, I can't pass. Didn't you hear me? I owe the guy for saving my life. You expect me to turn away from a fellow Marine? Bullshit partner, we're going down there, even if I have to whip your skinny ass, and throw you on that plane."

"And that's another thing, since when can you fly? Much less own four planes? I'm not flying with you, anywhere."

"I told you, I made a few dollars working for the new Angolan President and invested it in a cargo business. The guy that owned the planes and the routes got caught delivering cocaine instead of medicine and mail out in the Islands. I needed to scrub some of that payday cash from the President, so I set up an air cargo business out of Bogotá. We have contracts with little companies scattered throughout the

Caribbean to deliver goods and products. We also have a few inter-island mail routes. It's all legit, amigo."

"Yeah, but how'd you learn to fly in such a short time?

Do you even have a license? No instructor in their right mind would qualify you, Tom. I know your temper, and it doesn't mix with what I consider safe and courteous flying."

"Nah! That's all changed. Since Angola, I'm a pussycat. No more crazy stuff. And yes, I do have a pilot's license. I got it in Bogotá. It cost me ten large, but I got it."

"Swell! You *bought* your license in South America! Do they sell *brains* down there too?" Jack fumed.

"Hey Jacky, I ain't that dumb. I don't actually do the flying. I have pilots that do the work. I just go along to keep 'em honest, you know, make sure they don't go *poco loco* on me. Besides, I'm learning as I fly with them. I take over once we're up, and have landed a bunch of times. I haven't done any take-offs yet, but maybe tomorrow I'll try," he said with a grin.

"Look, Jack, let's just go down there and listen to what Austin has to say. We don't need to commit, or nothing. If it sounds too dangerous, or not in our line of work, we'll bounce, OK?"

"All right, Tom. It won't hurt to just listen, but remember, the first time I sniff anything that could get us in trouble, I'm out of there. Deal?"

"Deal."

Later that night, Jack was sitting on the porch, swinging gently back and forth, letting his brain float wherever it wanted to go. He found that if he did this often, all the bad things he had done in his life would mix in with all the good things and it all began to even out, kind of like a chocolate and vanilla swirl cake-batter. Sometimes, there were still lumps in the batter that just wouldn't dissolve no matter how hard he tried to stir. Lumps, like the shame of being drunk for three months,

His eyes closed and was drifting lazily on the sweet scent of jasmine and plumeria blossoms, little gecko feet were tap dancing across the underside of the tin roof defying gravity, huge stars were blinking bright through the swaying coconut palms. The sound of music and laughter drifted over from Duval Street. His eyes suddenly snapped open on full alert. Something moved out in the alley. He spotted a shadow fade into darker shadows. He sat still trying to pick up any movement. The shuffling sound came again from behind the fence, this time with a little grunt. Jack leapt up, did a one-handed jump over the fence, hoping it wasn't Donny's pit bull taking a crap. His leap was off target and landed at the feet of a huge black man who was down on all fours. Jack scared the man more than he scared himself. He grabbed the bigger man in a headlock and squeezed. It was like trying to hurt a tree trunk. Nothing gave.

"Who are you?" Jack yelled. "What are you doing sneaking around out here?" He knuckled down harder without any apparent pain to the man.

"I ain't sneak'n 'roun nowhere. I's watch'n," the man blubbered.

Jack loosened his grip. "Watching who?"

"You, Mr. Marsh. Mama Dey sent me over to watch out for you. She says trouble coming your way, and I supposed to warn you if I see it coming."

"What kind of trouble?"

"I don't know. She says I'll know when I see it. So far I ain't seen nothing, I guess," the huge man said, as he struggled to get on his feet. "Y'all scared me to def cumin over that fence like a Woo-Woo, Man! I tink I poo myself. Dat stinks something awful. Is dat me, or you?"

"A what? A Woo-Woo?" Jack said, as he felt the seat of his pants. '*Not me.*'

"Yes, Suh, A ghosty."

"Oh. Hey, I'm sorry, I just didn't know who it was hiding out behind the fence this time of night," Jack said, as he helped the guy up. "Go back, and tell Mama Dey that I'm fine, and I don't need someone watching out for trouble. If it comes, I'll take care of it."

"No, Suh, I can't. I'm in training. I got to do everything she says, or she send me back to New Iberia. If I go back there, I ain't never going to learn about the Shine. My mama says I got the Shine, but I just don't know how to use it, and only Mama Dey can teach me. Mama Dey, she my great-great auntie, and my mama say she got the strongest shine in the world. My mama say I got it strong, too, but I get everything confused up. Dead folks be alive, alive folk's dead, messages from the other side get all gobbledygook, angels tease me bout stuff. Sometimes I tink I better off just being me, stead of some Shiner," he said as he rubbed his head.

"Well, you can't stay out here. Come on up to the porch. You're going to scare Donny's pit bull when he comes out for his nightly stroll."

Jack led the way back up on the porch, went inside and poured a couple of iced teas from the pitcher in the refrigerator.

"What's your name?" Jack asked.

"Caldwell, Tyrone Caldwell. My mama says that's our slave name. Nobody know our real name. That lady in New Orleans, she says my name be *Ty Obi*. She knows Mama Dey from long time ago, and say my blood's Obi blood, go all the way back to *The Village*. Our people be the *Bakongo* in da old days. The *Bakongo* all blessed with the sight. Everybody in old Africa come see them for healing, and such. That is, until the devil come and wipe out all the people that got the sight. He only left the bad ones that do conjure and spells, and such. Only a few *Sighters* escaped off into the bush. That New Orleans lady say Mama Dey one of them, But Mr.

Marsh, how can that be? That be over tree- hunnerd years ago. Mmm, mm! Sho sound strange, don't it."

"Tyrone, it's damn strange, if you think about it. Mama Dey helped me sober up with some of her *helpers.* I was real sick, but I remember seeing this beautiful young girl dancing over me, buck naked, seemed like for hours. Whoever it was, or whatever it was, it sure cured me. So there must be something to it. It's way beyond my pay-grade."

"Yes Suh, I know 'xactly what you're saying. Sometimes I get so scared I don't know what to do—

"Do about what?" Claire said as she came through the gate.

Tyrone jumped at the sound of Claire's voice. His eyes got huge, and his mouth flopped open when Claire stepped up on the porch. He stood up, knocking his tea over, and back-stepped off the porch, tripping over a clump of flowers in the process.

"Yes ma'am, ain't nothing, nothing at all. We just admiring the night, that's all. I got to go, Jack. Pleased to meet ya," he stammered, almost genuflecting, "Pssst, Jack. She be one of them angels I talking about. Ain't going to be no trouble round here. Oh Lawdy, no trouble t'all," he said with a pie-sized grin, and hurried out the gate.

"What in the world? Who was that, Jack?" Claire asked, as she watched Tyrone hurry down the alley, sneaking looks over his shoulder.

"That was Tyrone Caldwell, my new friend, and Shiner-in-training," he said grinning.

""Shiner? What are you talking about?"

"Oh nothing, just one of Mama Dey's students she sent over to watch out for me," he said, suddenly feeling like someone was watching from the shadows beyond the gate.

"Ty, go on home now," he yelled, watching for the big man to step out of the shadows. Nothing moved. "Hmm, must be my imagination."

"Let's sit, and you can tell me again about being your girl," Claire said, plopping down on the swing.

"So, how was work tonight?" he asked, trying to redirect the conversation.

"Long and boring Now let's talk. When are you going to tell me that you love me, that you can't possibly live without me, and that you will take me away from this island paradise? Hmm, when," she said with a leering smile on her face.

"Claire, I... uh, crap. Yes, to everything you just said, except double, all right? You finally got it out of me. Are you happy now?" he said defensively, sure that his face was the color of a big red balloon.

He felt giddy, like the time he accidently on purpose brushed up against Mrs. Campbell's breasts in the seventh grade. He almost fainted from the adrenaline rush he got from touching those beauties. Well, not actually *touching*, but more like a nano-second's brushing, Oh, but the joy. Up until this moment, Briar had been the most secret and wonderful person in his life, but now, sitting next to this woman, he was sure that his life was just beginning..."

"Jack? Jack, are you ok? You drifted away for a minute there, come back to me. You were about to tell me that you love me."

"I love you, Claire Marlow."

The tall thin man with the dreadlocks stood watching the couple on the porch from behind a huge gumbo limbo tree across the alley. He had seen and heard enough to report back to Jacque Lapin in Kingston. Jacques said he would pay him double if the information was solid, but he also said that if it turned out to be bullshit, he would kill the man. Everybody knows you don't fuck with Jacques. The Jamaican had driven down from Miami a few days ago, and had watched Marsh's every move. Discreetly checking around, he had learned about Marsh's experience with that old witch, Dey-something-or-other. He knew where the white chick worked and her schedule coming and going, and now he knew about Marsh and his friend's plans to fly to Kingston and meet with a guy named Burke in the morning. This had to be the information Jacques was looking for. The man slipped away from the huge tree and started down the alley, fishing his cell phone out of a cargo pocket. He spotted a large pit bull sniffing his way down the alley towards him. He did a quick U-turn, climbed up a tree and sat, watching as the animal did its business and trotted back up the alley.

CHAPTER 5

The Cessna Caravan descended on a long smooth glide path towards the most spectacular silver-green water in the Caribbean. The pontoons hit the emerald waters off Point Royal, bounced a couple of times before settling down on the calm waters, and motored over to the customs pier to check in with the local constabulary.

The flight down from Key West had been nerve jostling in the single engine prop plane, especially when an old Soviet era Mig 19 fighter plane came alongside when they were over Cuba, hanging wing-tip to wing-tip until the Cessna cleared Cuba's airspace. The jet pilot waved a friendly good bye as the old Cuban trainer peeled off. Tom said that there wasn't any hassle because his four planes all had Columbian markings and numbers, plus all his pilots spoke Spanish.

Everything had been going fine until Ernie, the pilot, a pony-tailed guy with bad teeth, flipped the motor's switch to off, pushed the wheel forward, and folded his arms in mock-death.

"*Heart Attack!*" He screamed loud enough to shake the windscreen. Tom went into immediate action. He hit a couple of switches, feathered the engines, and pulled the descending plane up and back on course. All of this took less than a minute, but it was the longest minute of Jack's life.

"Tom, Ernie, for as long as you two know me, don't *ever*, *ever* do that again. Is that clear?" he demanded, wanting to smack them both in the back of their heads.

"Chill out, Bro. That was one of my flight lessons. I told all my guys to put us in serious trouble whenever it was safe to. That's the only way to learn the real deal, Jack," Tom said, as he chewed on a nasty cigar stub, and piloted the aircraft like an old salt.

A policeman stamped their passports while one of his men checked the plane out for contraband and drugs. Jamaica's reputation for being a drug crossroads for narcotics to the U.S. is well earned. A huge portion of the local economy relied on the money the trade generates. Tourism is a distant second to drugs, with most visitors sequestered behind hotel walls and security fences for their safety. The term, 'All Inclusive', was invented by the travel industry and is usually a signal that the destination may not be safe outside of the resort's perimeter. The local police have a zero-tolerance for the island people buying, selling, or using any form of drugs, but its use is so prevalent that they just turn a blind eye to it and let street gangs do pretty much whatever they want to do.

Austin Burke was waiting in front of the customs building for them to come out. He grabbed Tom in a big bear hug and lifted him off his feet.

"God dammit, Tom, you look good. Retirement must be treating you right," Austin said, holding Tom off at arm's length.

"You're looking pretty good yourself, Lieutenant. Still a bed-wetter?" Tom said, joking as he ducked a big roundhouse punch.

"Bullshit, Corporal. You can't talk to an officer and a gentleman like that, and besides, it ain't none of your business if I do or I don't. Come on, let's get out of this sun. I got a car over here," Austin said as he led them to a Land Cruiser.

An hour later, they were aboard the *Sea Bird Explorer*, anchored off Port Royal in a little bay about fifty feet deep that was topaz green and clear enough to drink.

"Tiny, bring up that sounding again, cut back on all the sea noises, and give us the pure sonar return," Austin said,

"Aye-aye, Skipper." The Explorer's captain answered. He was also the ship's pilot, as well as the electronics tech aboard. The other three crewmembers were either ashore or back in the States for a brief R&R.

The echoes didn't mean anything to Jack, as they *pinged* and *ponged* over the instrument's recording device. Austin could see from his and Tom's expression that they didn't know what they were supposed to be hearing.

"The ping that you hear is the bounce-back of a soundwave we send down to see what the bottom looks like.

It also tells us many other things, like the makeup of the sea floor, the thickness of the crust to a limited degree, any subsurface abnormalities. It's these abnormalities that we look for. We get the right kind of ping back and we can pretty much tell what's lying on the floor," Austin said. "That's an over-simplification of it, but when you put together a lot of other factors like strata, pressure vents, satellite data, it all starts to tell us what's down there," Austin said as he sat down on a stool next to the chart table.

"For years I have been working these Caribbean waters, the Gulf of Mexico, Central and South America. I have always been fascinated by the irregularity of the seabed in this area, but because of technology and exploration limitations, I just tucked it away for someday when I could investigate the area."

"Austin, it sounds like you've been a busy boy since being a boot lieutenant in the Marine Corps, back in the day," Tom said.

"Six years was enough. I could have stayed in for twenty, but my first love was calling. I have treasure in my veins, just like my daddy. Hell Tom, I was raised on a deck, shuttling from one dive site to the next. I got out of the Corps and picked up right where my old man left off. I've made a ton of money, and I've lost a ton. I'm after what old Mother Nature is hiding from us. I want to know her secrets, and I want to know her hiding places, where her treasure troves are," Austin said with a dreamer's glint in his eye.

"So, this *ping, pong* we're hearing is what, Cortez's Holy Grail?" Jack asked. He didn't know why he was being so defensive about this whole meeting. Maybe it was because he could smell trouble in the air. His sixth sense was kicking in and he recalled what Mama Dey said about fire and water coming his way.

"Look, I'm sorry for my remarks. I'm just coming off a bad time in my life, and I'm usually not such an asshole. Tell me what you think I can do to help you with whatever it is you're doing."

"What exactly have you found, Austin?" Tom asked.

"Five billion dollars in gold," Austin said, as if it was the most natural thing a guy could say. He almost looked apologetic for finding it.

"Excuse me?" Jack said in astonishment. "Did you say five billion?"

"Yes, you heard correctly. Every ounce was stolen out of the Venezuelan treasury by Hugo Chavez and was being transported to Havana for safe keeping."

Jack sat down on a stool trying to comprehend what he had just heard. When the U.S. national debt blew by twenty trillion, the world gasped as Wall Street rubbed its greedy paws together. Then when McDonalds served it's billionth Big Mac, fat people rejoiced, and when oil hit a hundred and forty bucks a barrel the Arabs beat their wives in pure ecstasy. But this! This was trouble, big trouble, life-ending trouble, Jack Marsh gets killed trouble. His little pea-brain couldn't even comprehend what Austin had just told them. His bowels signaled to get ready for a bad case of monkey butt. Jim Beam was calling loud. *'Time to scoot, Boot!'*

He sat dumbfounded for a moment, and then his capitalist's mind kicked in.

"Who all knows about this, Austin? You, the crew, who else?" Jack was beginning to feel the old stir for adventure in his gut. He needed to be back in the game, but he held back from committing just yet.

"Just me and the crew, and of course, Dick Chandler, my senior oceanographer, and now you two. That's why I contacted you, I knew you had experience in major recoveries like this one and that I could trust you. Believe me when I tell you this is a powder keg we're sitting on. If we don't handle this correctly, we could all disappear."

"Where is your crew now?"

"You met Tiny. I gave the other three guys a few days off to go home and take care of personal business. One of the guys lives here in Kingston, the other two in Galveston. We've been gone for over three months; they have families to take care of. I didn't see anything wrong with letting them go. They've all been with me for years," Austin said, defending his men against any suspicion.

"What about Chandler, where is he?"

"Dick? He flew back to Houston to start doing the paperwork. Texas A&M has an excellent maritime school in Galveston that he can use for source material. We're ninety-nine percent positive of our find, and the size of it, but Dick is a stickler for dotting eyes and crossing t's. In fact, I should have heard back from him by now. It's not like him to not stay in touch," Austin said, with little worry lines forming around his eyes.

"Tiny, call Dick's Houston number, and let's see what he found out."

"Will do, Skipper," Tiny said, as he went into the radio room.

"Austin, you should have Tiny recall the other crew members too, get them all back on board for now. With this kind of a find you need to hold everything close in," Tom said. "What about the data? Does anyone have copies, other than Chandler in Houston?"

"No. everything is right here in these computers. I printed out various synopses and analyses, but nothing that can be interpreted without more information. Any satellite imagery that is out there could show our tracks over the last couple of months. But as long as no one knows what it is we found they wouldn't be concerned with knowing where to look. The wreck is in a cylinder-shaped crevice on the seabed's floor, so unless you have pretty tight GPS numbers you won't know where to look. "

"In your call the other day to Tom, you said that your preliminary guess on the amount of gold may be low. Five billion doesn't sound narrow to me," Jack said.

"That was an initial estimate. When the news came out about a missing submarine, it was reported to all maritime traffic that it was a Cuban sub on routine patrol that had gone down. Then when reports of Chavez's death started leaking out of Maracaibo, it was also rumored that a submarine loaded with the entire Venezuelan national gold reserves was missing. U.S. sources quickly debunked that using known facts. Venezuelan reserves were estimated to be a hundred-plus billion in gold. The old November Class nuclear sub is not capable of carrying that much weight. It would sink pier-side. The max it would be able to carry would be between three billion and six billion dollars in gold bullion. So to be conservative, I'm saying five billion, anything more than that is gravy."

"Where is the sub located, Austin?" Tom asked.

They gathered around the chart table as Austin spread his calipers apart, and walked them down from Kingston to a spot the size of a tiny pinhole on the chart.

"14.00° N, 76°.20 W, plus or minus a few meters. It has been down there for four years, rusting, expanding, contracting, growing a living skin of microscopic sea life that will eventually crush the hull. Left to the sea, the current will fill in the crevice with sand and rubble hiding the treasure for all time. Now that we have found it, every scavenger and salvager in the world is going to be on top of the wreck."

Jack believed in never picking a fight, but he also wouldn't run from one either as long as the odds were in his favor. The retrieval of the gold wouldn't be tough, it was just a matter of punching a hole in the hull and hauling the gold topside. What had Jack worried were all the freebooters who were going to descend on the place like tiger sharks in a feeding frenzy. He still had doubts about whether he wanted to really be part of the operation or not. He wanted some time to think it over.

"So, Tom, don't we have a plane to catch?" he asked

"We ain't going anywhere, yet. Not until Austin tells us what he needs us for," Tom said looking over to his old platoon commander.

"Austin, how can we help? Lay it out; if it's something we can do, we'll sign on."

"Thanks, Tom, I knew I could count on you. And Jack, just so you know, it wasn't me who saved your buddy's ass in Fallujah. It's the other way around. Tom picked my skinny ass up and carried me, shooting over his shoulder at the muzzies all the way back to the highway, then ran back and hauled out two other guys that were pinned down. When I thanked him later for saving my life he told me, *'Shut the fuck up, Burke, you bled all over my last Cohiba, you Motherfucker.'* Austin laughed at the memory, although at the time he had a hole in his stomach from an AK round.

"Uh oh, I see it coming, the old Band of Brothers guilt trip." Jack said under his breath.

"I sort of figured it was something like that. Tom has a way of getting people into dangerous situations and then saving their ass. His brother told me it was because he was so ugly as a child, the other kids would throw rocks at him. He would pay the schoolyard bully to start a fight with the kids and then he would jump in and save them at the last minute so he could be a hero."

"Bullshit. Jack. Austin, don't listen to him. He'll go along with whatever you and I agree to, or I'll whip *his* ass."

"Ok, let me lay it out. Secrecy and security are my two main concerns. I am not exaggerating when I say once word gets out, and I know it will, many men will die before the first gold brick breaks the surface. Jack, you have recovered a couple of major finds yourself and know that going down and getting the gold back up is going to be just basic salvage recovery work. The problem as I see it is going to be security during the recovery, and then once we have it all up, getting it to the nearest U.S. port. I estimate it will take about a week to transfer the gold out of the wreck and lift it topside."

"Lifting that much weight over that short a period of time is going to require eight to ten divers, a recompression chamber, rest time, limited bottom time," Jack said, thinking outload. "It can't be done, Austin. You need more time and more divers."

"We don't have either one, Jack. We need to scoop up the gold and disappear in the wind."

"You guys aren't thinking. Thank God for gunnery sergeants," Tom said. "Let's get the Hughes people on the horn and get them to lease us the *Glomar Explorer*. We could drop the claws down and scoop up the whole frigging submarine. Last I heard it was tied up in Mobile's shipyard rusting."

"My God, Tom. Believe it or not I had the same idea the other day. The only problem is, it was sold to a Chinese salvage yard a few years ago as scrap. Of course, the C.I.A. still has a tight hold on that entire operation. I have a friend upstairs at Hughes where Operation Azorean is still thought of as a major cold war coup by the Agency and the board members as the biggest heist ever pulled on the high seas. The Russians are still convinced that they brought up the K-129 intact. The Agency has always admitted to bringing up only the front one-third of the sub. Who knows what the truth is?"

Jack snapped his fingers, "Forget Hughes. I can get us something just as good and it won't involve screwing with the C.I.A. Those bastards would steal the gold from us in a heartbeat."

"Talk to me, son." Austin's eyes were sparkling green as he leaned across the chart table and squeezed Jack's arm.

"I have a friend that hauls pipe out of Cameron, Louisiana to the offshore rigs. The boat is basically comparable to the *Glomar*. The bottom opens up similar to a bomb bay door on the old B52's There is a huge crane on the bow and one amidships. Drill platforms are going up so fast out in the Gulf that the demand for pipe is a twenty-four-seven problem. Shell, B.P. and a few other big companies have sunk holding racks on the seafloor. The delivery boat drops the pipe into the pens and the platforms bring them up as needed.

"That's the darndest thing I've ever heard of, Jack." Austin was nodding his head. "We could drop anchor over the sub, lower lifting cables, and bring the whole sub up. Damn! I like it. It's a much better plan than sending divers down. I say we go with it"

"There's a third option," Jack said, earnestly.

Both men looked over at him with questioning looks.

"Let's seal the crevice up and get the hell out of here. And on the way out, destroy every trace and record of the location and what's down there. On a scale of one to five, I would mark this a ten. People are going to die. there's just too much money down there. I say we shake hands and call it a day," he said sincerely, meaning every word.

CHAPTER 6

The dusty streets of Spanish Town on the outskirts of Kingston are the island's most notorious and dangerous area to live, much less visit. The murder per-capita rate is the highest on the Island and is in the running with Juarez, Mexico as being the most violent. Most killings are done by "*Shotta's*" and the majority of the victims are innocent by-standers, children, women, and old men. The targets are rival

Yardies, gang members, or *Rude Boys* out killing, just to be out killing. Blasts from AK 47's, Uzi's, and Mac 10's are as common as firecrackers at a Chinese funeral. Drug importing and exporting is the number one commercial business on the Island and there are dozens of competing *Posses* that are ruthless in their drive to be the most powerful drug gang on the Island.

The sun had set and dark was coming on. Tiny Miles made his way up Stone Street in Spanish Town in search of Lamont Troupe, the *Sea Bird Explorer's* chief engineer. Calls to Lamont's cell phone went unanswered and unreturned. After a dozen calls, Tiny decided he would go fetch Lamont. He supposed Lamont was laid up drunk at his mother's house again. Most port lay-overs would find Lamont broke after a few days of binge drinking, ready to come back aboard to sweat out the Heebie- Jeebies, as he called them. The rose-red painted house with the tin roof was just as Tiny remembered it from his last visit. The yard was small and bare of a single blade of grass or weed. A few scrawny chickens pecked around nervously in search of any morsel before it got much darker. After dark, the dogs come out and any chicken found outside its coop was a goner. The chickens knew this, and hurriedly pecked at Tiny's feet as he went up the porch steps.

"Hello the house," Tiny hailed. "Lamont, it's me Tiny, you in there," he said loudly, as he squinted through the screen door.

"What you want, whitey mon?" A deep voice said from the dark interior.

"Yes, Ma'am, It's me, Tiny Miles from the *Sea Bird Explorer*. Captain Austin asked me to fetch Lamont back aboard. Is he home?"

"He home, all right. Come on in and see for yourself," a huge woman said, as she unlatched the screen door and held it open for Tiny, shooing flies as they swarmed to get in.

"Go onto the back bedroom, he back there."

Tiny walked through the small kitchen and into the dimly lit back bedroom. Lamont was laid out, still dressed in the same clothes he wore when he left the ship over a week ago.

"Lamont, come on buddy, we gotta get back to the *Sea Bird*, we're sailing soon," Tiny said, and gave Lamont's arm a tug. The arm didn't move. It was stiff as a board, *'The fuck!'*

"Lamont?" Tiny said alarmed.

"He can't hear you none. He dead, been dead a week. My Lamont, been dead a week," Mrs. Troupe cried out. "He come home one night, out drinking, blabbing his mouth off to everybody, about something secret y'all found, make everybody rich, and got his gizzard cut open. He said that Jacques Lapin hurt him bad, and made him tell everything about what y'all found out there on the Blue. He says Lapin hurt him so bad, he told that devil what the secret was, and who all Mr. Austin told, and who they are, and everything about what's down there. My Lamont so proud bout what all y'all found, said it was going to make us rich. He said Captain Burke done called in two of his friends that are experts in something or other from Key West, mon named Marsh to help out protecting it from the world." The distraught woman wept, "Then when Jacques pushed Lamont for the location he told him he don't know exactly, but the information is on the boat. Then that devil Lapin stuck a shucken knife into my baby's gut so he would die. Now what I supposed to do? My boy dead, I ain't got nothing now. How I gonna live?"

"Mrs. Troupe, I'm sure Mr. Burke had some insurance on Lamont, don't you worry. Meanwhile, I think we ought to get Lamont over to a funeral home, or someplace to have him taken care of."

"I sent word for Miss Oola, she be along soon. She thinks maybe we bring him back if we can catch him soon enough."

"Excuse me, ma'am, bring who back?" Tiny said confused.

"Lamont. But, she better hurry, it already been a week. He might slip by. Miss Oola, she powerful, but a week is a long time. He come back after too long, could be trouble."

"Uh, Mrs. Troupe, have you notified the authorities about Lamont's murder?"

"Authorities! Me? They ain't caring about one more dead mon, or no murder. Besides, most' em work for that Jacques Lapin. He evil. You see this dog paw on this here string round my neck. Dat one powerful juju, the rest of that dog out hunting for Lapin. When that dog finds him, he kill him quick, and then eat him slow. Dat be my justice."

"Well, I sure don't know anything about that, but I do know that Lamont needs some proper care, Mrs. Troupe. He's already starting to go bad, if you'll excuse my saying so."

"He be fine, as soon as Miss Oola get here. She coming from Ocho Rios, the other side of the Island. It not that far, but she got lots of commitments and can't just drop everything, but if she say she come, she come."

"All right then, I guess I'll just go on back and report to Mr. Burke about Lamont. I'm sure he'll want to come by to pay his respects, and see what he can do for you. Lamont was a good man and we'll sure miss him, ma'am."

"I know Lamont going to miss working on that boat. You tell Mr. Austin he can come by anytime, I'll be here. And y'all be careful going back down to town, you never know when one of them *Yardies* start shoot'n and yelling them dirty words," Mrs. Troupe said, as she dabbed at her eyes.

Across the dusty road from the red shack, a young man on a motor scooter sat and watched the *Whitey Mon* come down the stairs, and start down the street towards town. The boy's instructions were to watch Lamont's house and report on any visitors or police that come by. He figured that this had to be important enough that he could leave his post to follow the stranger to see where he went. Jacques Mon liked initiative in his *Yardies,* as long as it paid out in useful news. If it turned into nothing, then the *Yardie* could get a serious ass-whooping by Jacques's personal *Shottas.* The young man kick-started the ancient Vespa and slowly pulled out from his hide as the big Whitey Mon reached the far corner.

Ten minutes later, a small child-like figure approached the gate to the red house with an open umbrella over her shoulder, and a small valise in her hand. She nudged the gate open with a small barefoot and entered the yard. Three mangy yard-dogs caught sight of her and slinked off around the side yard, tails tucked tight to their rumps. The front door opened wide, with Mrs. Troupe silhouetted by dim candle light.

"Thank God! Oola Dey, I knew you come. They done stabbed and killed my boy. Before he died he told me he know a secret bigger than the whole world, that going to make us all richer than the Newnited States," Mrs. Troupe said raising her arms in praise. "He says he can't die yet, he got to tell somebody in the guv'ment."

"I'm here to tend your boy, maybe try to catch his spirit before it too late, Sister Ritha," the tiny woman said as she entered the shack.

Oola Dey suddenly stopped, "I hear whispering, Ritha, somebody scared and crying-out the other side. Something about bloody murder 'n drowning. I don't understand. We better get to work, hurry. Bring some of that salve I told you to make, and put that dog foot away for now. We going to need something stronger than that to catch this spirit," she said, as she pulled out a small skull, perhaps a monkey's, or maybe a child's, yellowed with age. "And go pee in a jar, we going to need lots for sure. I feeling a house full of spirits swooshing around," she said, throwing a handful of white coconut powder around the room, clucking rhythmically, while strutting around Lamont's bed like a hen, elbows out and flapping.

The dogs outside started to cry, and howl out of fear, sensing unseen guests up in the trees.

Across town, on Kingston's East Side, the streets off the main thoroughfare are narrow and crowded with vendor stalls and small shops, selling everything from fruits and vegetables, to clothing and electronics, almost like an open air Wal-Mart. Shoppers keep a wary eye out for cars, motorbikes, trucks, bicycles, and the occasional donkey-drawn cart. The noise is a mix of island reggae, rap, lilting Jamaican English, hawkers, dogs, and kids.

Off Cane and Boot Streets there is a compound that covered an entire square block with high walls made of cinderblock and painted a bright yellow running around it. Every flat surface in these back streets had graffiti scribbling and local-life murals painted on them, except for the yellow wall surrounding Jacques "Dada" Lapin's home and business compound. The compound is like a fortress with a front gate and a back gate. The exterior walls are topped with concertina razor wire, security cameras are mounted around the perimeter, and monitored at all times. Armed men patrol the grounds, protecting their leader. Every few yards, a *juju* is tacked to the walls to ward off evil spirits.

Lapin, to the outside world, was seen as *the* criminal kingpin in Jamaica's underworld. His gang is known as DaDa's Posse, the largest and most ruthless on the Island, with subsidiary Posses in Miami, New York, and throughout the Caribbean. His largest source of income was from drugs coming from Venezuela, protected by his special relationship with President Maduro. Some of the drugs stayed on the Island to feed the locals, while the rest was sucked north to the U.S. and the U.K.

In spite of all the competition from the Mexican cartels, business was good, and growing. The alarming trend however, was the growing drug addiction of the Caribbean people. With brutal poverty and diseases infecting the Islands, and agriculture and commerce shrinking. the largest export throughout the Islands was the island people themselves. People were crowding boats to escape to a better life to anywhere but where they were. Most don't make it, illegal immigration enforcement had increased a hundredfold since 9-11, many drowned, or were killed for their meager possessions, and others made it to the states, but lived in the shadows. No better off than where they came from.

Lapin fancied himself the Savior of his island, Jamaica, and the Caribbean itself. He was generous with his money, and gave freely to orphanages, country schools, and the poor. Much of his generosity was motivated by his belief and upbringing in the ancient African religions that the slaves brought over to the new world. The basis of the belief was founded in witchcraft, mysticism, and spirit worship. His mother was a well-known powerful diviner and voodoo shaman in the small towns in the mountains. Jacques was raised on dark rituals, castings, spells, often serving as an acolyte to his Mother for fetching's and exorcisms. Jacques gained an unhealthy fear of the Dark Side through his upbringing, and was extremely superstitious. but still, he worked both sides of the spirit world to his advantage, both good deeds and evil deeds.

Years ago, he had visited the Island's most famous mystic, Oola Dey, to find out what he could about himself regarding his beginnings and his future. Sister Oola ran her hands and fingers across his head and face, touching, stopping, humming. She placed her index fingers in his ears and her thumbs in his nostrils, and cocked an ear as if listening to someone.

"You Kakwa clan," Oola Dey proclaimed, appearing to be off somewhere else.

"Up north somewhere, maybe even farther than Uganda, your old people named Dada. Your family women wear black head to foot. I feel hunger and death, fighting and crying flying through time. I see part of your family turn white, the other part with knives turn the same color as the night. A woman calling me, named Suki something, her son powerful. The people call him, 'Lord of the Beasts,' and hate him. He is given a holy name from the teachings of the usurper Prophet. His name is Idi Amin. He is in your blood." Oola's head snapped up, and she pulled her hands away from Jacques, as if she had touched a hot plate.

"Mister Jacques, your road going to be a long one, mostly rough and unclear. Nothing is free for you, you will take it, and become powerful like your relative. Be careful; don't make the people hate you. If you take, you got to give, if you hate, you must also love. Men going to fear you, and try to kill you. Watch your back, always. I see money and power, Mister Jacques, but I see death all around you. Your Mama has a very dark following on the other side, and she going to try to help you by using them black spirits. There are many on the other side that want loose, and they going to try to use you to break out of the river that eats all rivers. Please go now," she said, abruptly leaving the room.

Lapin believed everything that the old "Shiner" had told him and quickly read everything he could about his Ugandan Cousin. He quickly added Dada to his name, and demanded his gang members use it as a show of respect for his African clan. He genuinely believed that his future was to rule the Caribbean Islands. To accomplish this, he needed money. The recent treasure find was going to be his war chest. Nothing could, or would stop him now, at least on this side of the wall.

CHAPTER 7

The crew quarters aboard the *Sea Bird Explorer* were spacious compared to some of the Navy's troopships that Tom had been on during his time in the Marines. Hell, the bunk even had a mattress on it, not just a piece of canvas lashed to a pipe frame. From the porthole he could see Kingston all lit up across the Bay with the mountains off in the distance silhouetting the Island from the millions of stars sparkling above. It was a beautiful sight. It reminded him of Manila's night-lights, back when the Philippine's was like a wild west town that never slept.

Tom took in the city lights off in the distance, but his real focus was on a low riding speedboat idling off a hundred meters from the *Sea Bird*. It had been off the portside for a couple of hours holding station. Three men aboard her took turns watching the *Sea Bird* through binoculars. The boat had shown up shortly after Tiny came back aboard with the news about Lamont having been murdered by some local drug lord because of what he knew about the sunken treasure. Jack and Austin had left for the airport an hour earlier than Tiny's return back aboard.

The plan was for Austin to get back to Houston and find Dick Chandler. He also needed to meet with his investors to try to finagle a little more money from them to pay for the lift boat. It was going to be a tough sell. Austin hated having to lie to his friends about some bogus *find* that may yield enough for everyone to break even, but not much more. When in truth, the gold could make each of them rich beyond the richest Texas oil baron. It could also put them right in the middle of a Caribbean free-for-all, to see who could gain control of Chavez's treasure, as he had begun to call it. Tom thought that Jack's idea to bury the sub in the crevice and let it lay undiscovered was the smartest thing to do, given the trouble it was sure to bring down on everyone trying to get control of the prize.

Tom called Jack on his cell phone, hoping to get him before he caught a plane back to the U.S. It had been agreed that while Austin would try to get financing to lease the lift boat, Jack would contact his friend in Florida's Bureau of Investigation and tell him what they had discovered. They felt this would give them some official type of cover if things went bad in recovering the treasure. The rationale was that the Florida cops could keep a secret and it would protect Jack, Tom, and Austin if the news ever got out. Jack was counting on Captain Bill Price to know what to do with the information. If he couldn't trust Bill, there was no one he could trust. Bill was a stand-up guy and was also madly in love with Coco Duvalier, Jack's partner in the Sand Bar.

"Hey, what's up?" Jack answered, after a couple of rings. He was on stand-by for a flight to Miami in thirty minutes on Air Jamaica. Austin had lucked out and caught a coach-seat on a Continental flight to Houston, and was probably at cruising altitude by now.

"Jackie, I'm glad I caught you before you sky-out. Listen, Tiny returned from Lamont's house and found that he had been murdered almost a week ago. Some local gang-banger cut him open trying to find out all the details of what Austin has found. The really bizarre part is that Lamont's mother still has his body at home, waiting for some witch doctor to show up to do some kind of last rights, or something."

"Oh man, that is weird," Jack said, flashing back on a vision of some nubile maiden dancing over him. "Tom, I have a bad feeling about all this leaking out somehow, and right now we're sitting right in the middle of it."

"Yeah well, that ain't all. We have one of those druggy speedboats you hear about that can outrun an RPG sitting off our port bow as we speak. Three Rasta looking dudes are scoping us out with night vision goggles. So far, they're just looking, but Tiny and I are on a hundred percent alert for any touchy-feely stuff," Tom said, as he peeked out of his porthole again.

"Can you get the immigration cops over to take a look? Maybe chase them off."

"Nah! We can handle them if they try any funny stuff," Tom said. "I just wanted you to know about Lamont's murder before you get in the air. I told Austin I would baby-sit his boat until he gets back, so rest assured I am not letting anybody fuck with it while I'm in charge."

"I don't like this a damn bit, Tom. I knew we were going to get our ass in a sling the minute I heard about Austin needing help, Keeryst! Chandler's missing, Lamont's murdered, gangbangers are involved, who the fuck else is out there?"

"You know Jack, I hate to agree with you, but you may be right about us being a little out of our league on this one. Let's stick it out until Austin gets back with his equipment, then we'll bow out. Meanwhile, talk to your cop friend. Tell him what's going on. I think he needs to get a heads-up on this one."

"I've got a connecting flight out of Miami up to Tallahassee tonight so I should be able to get in to see Captain Price first thing," Jack said. "After I finish up with Price, I'm going back to Key West for a few days to get my business back in order. I'll be there if you need me, just call and I'll be down on the next flight, OK?"

"You worry too much, amigo. The Rasta dude ain't been made yet that I'm going to need any help on," Tom said with a sneering laugh.

"Tom, I wasn't thinking about some Rasta dude. I'm thinking more like some Nicaraguan dudes, or some Venezuelan dudes, maybe a few Cuban dudes, or Mexican cartel dudes, or some dynamite-ass-strapped ISIS dude. You know, the serious guys, hell, maybe even some CIA dudes."

"You know my motto, Jack. When the situation is in doubt, *Run like hell*. How do you think I've lived this long? An old Master Sergeant taught me a long time ago that *Fight or Flight* was for cavemen. The new rule is Pee *and Flee.*"

"Try to remember those pearls of wisdom, okay? They're calling my flight, have to go, I'll call you from Key West," Jack said, and hung up.

An hour later, Tom was sitting in the wheelhouse in the Skipper's chair, chewing on a cold cigar. It was after two in the morning and the speedboat was still off the port bow, idling in a low deep rumble. Tiny had cut off all shipboard lights earlier and was snoring softly, curled up on the deck next to the bank of radios. Austin's dog, Daisy was lying next to Tiny with her four paws up in the air, one of them was cutting the cheese every few minutes, and the pilothouse was getting downright nasty.

Tom went out on the bow for fresh air and a stretch when the speedboat's motor rumbled a pitch higher. Tom dropped down behind the gunwale and peeked over the side. The boat was coming about making a heading for the *Sea Bird*. Tom scrambled back to the pilothouse and shook Tiny awake. Daisy was up sniffing the air with hackles all prickly sensing trouble.

A tall thin man grabbed the railing on the port side and swung aboard the deck soundlessly. A second man followed a few seconds later. Both men were carrying automatic machine pistols of some type, holding them at the ready, their heads swiveling and bobbing as they looked for the two men that they knew were aboard. Daisy let out a deep throated growl, and the men froze. Tiny stepped out of a hatchway and shot one of the men with a spear gun from three feet away. The man dropped his pistol, grabbed his chest, and tried to pull the barbed shaft out as he sank to his knees and pitched forward. Tiny nailed the second man in the shoulder with another steel-barbed bolt that knocked him back against the bulkhead. Tiny stepped forward and hit the man across the forehead with the spear gun, knocking him unconscious.

Tom jumped from the top of the wheelhouse, down into the speedboat, landing on the boat's skipper with his full weight. Tom heard the whoosh of air from the guy's lungs and squeezed his windpipe closed with a steel grip. The man's eyes bulged as his brain screamed for air. His hands tried to break the hold that was killing him. Tom held tight for a few more seconds then punched the guy in the nose as hard as he could, and let go his chokehold. The man slumped back, semi-conscious, gasping for air. Tom tied off the speedboat to the *Sea Bird*, hoisted his man over the railing, and let him flop around like a Nassau Grouper on the deck. Daisy came over, snapping at the flopping figure, sure the squirming man was going to be given to her to play with.

After completely stripping the three men, Tiny and Tom lowered them into the aft hold back by the engine compartment, then dogged it down. It was a tight fit for all three with diesel fumes filling the air and heat from the auxiliary motor chugging away at over a hundred degrees. While Tiny hosed the bloody deck down with a pressure hose, Tom searched the speedboat for any weapons or papers. He wrapped a bungee cord round the helm then cinched it tight around the seat frame, locking the wheel in place. He repositioned the throttle up a few notches and the powerful motor growled and strained at its tether. Back aboard *Sea Bird*, Tom pulled the line around to get the speedboat's bow pointed at Kingston and let loose the painter line. The Speedboat immediately took off in a straight beeline at about ten knots for the city lights across the harbor.

At daybreak, they hoisted the anchor and made their way out of Point Royal without any attention. Just one more boat in the parade of lobstermen, fishing charters, dive boats, and small inter-island cargo ships. The sun was at their back on a west by north-west course of 285° making for the Cayman Islands. While Jamaica was still in sight, Tiny throttled back to idle speed as Tom un-dogged the cargo hold, motioned for the two men to climb out, and to bring the dead man with them. Daisy took one sniff of the stiffening corpse and slunk off, looking back over her shoulder. The man with the spear gun barb in his shoulder was in a lot of pain and weak from loss of blood. The dude with the bruised windpipe and broken nose couldn't have been more talkative.

"It was not our plan to hurt you white mons. We just wanted to get the location of the treasure place," the skinny man said in a heavily accented English-Jamaican singsong lilt. "DaDa Lapin said he would kill us if we did not have the information back to him before daybreak."

"Jody Mon, shut your mouth," the wounded man said. "You getting us killed for sure. This white devil going to kill us just like he killed Marcus here," he said as he nudged the corpse at his feet. "Back off, and shut you up, Mon."

"Don't you worry Stinky Mon, these whites not kill us already, they not kill us now," Jody said, as he looked at Tom for agreement.

"Nah! We ain't going to kill you. We're going to let the sharks take care of you."

"*What you say Mon? Sharks!*" Jody cried out, "Don't do that to us, Mon."

"Just kidding," Tom said laughing. "We're going to put you in a rubber boat, and you can paddle back. Hell, it's only three or four miles, you two lads will be home in time for lunch."

"No Sir, we can't go back. DaDa Lapin kill us for sure. Marcus is dead, speedboat she gone, and we don't have the location of the treasure spot. We be dead before the noonday gun blow at Point Royal," Jody said, clearly concerned about his immediate future. "I think it best for our health if we stay your prisoners, Boss Mon"

"You're nuts. Last night you guys were going to kill us. Now you want us to save your skinny butts. No way. Slip your drawers on, and get ready to go over the side," Tom said, as he kicked the pile of clothes over to them.

Tiny came out of the wheel house pulling Tom off to the side,

"Maybe this is our chance to throw this Lapin character off the scent. Let's have Jody report into Lapin on the cell phone with the bogus map-grid numbers Jack came up with, 15.00N / 80°W. Give Lapin some story about hiding aboard the *Sea Bird*."

"Tiny, you're a genius. Put the bad coordinates out there and any other characters that show up will be working with the same data," Tom said laughing at the ruse. He grabbed Jody by his arm and pulled him inside the wheel house.

"Okay, Jody, we have decided we will let you guys live, but this is what you have to do...."

After several trial runs, Jody had the story down tight. He took a big slug of water, and hit *send* on his cell,

."Jacques DaDa, this be Jody Mon. Listen mon, I got to talk fast. Me and Stinky hiding on the white mon's boat, Marcus dead, the speedboat she is gone somewhere. Me and Stinky kill one white mon and make him talk before he die. You write this down, Boss Mon, fifteen period, nothing, nothing, big N, then below that write, eight nothing, real little nothing on top of big nothing, big W. You got all that, DaDa Mon?" Jody asked as he wiped sweat from his upper lip.

"This don't make sense, Yardie. You smoking some my ganja, Mon? Get your ass back here so I can look you in the eye, see if you lying to me. You be lying, you dead."

"I swear, DaDa Boss, I'm not lying. It's the truth. Besides, I think me and Stinky going to have to shoot our way out of here. That's the only way we going to make it back," Jody said with a catch in his throat, really getting into the act. "If you don't see us again, that be okay, Jacques DaDa. We be part of your Posse forever, even the other side," Jody finished weeping loudly.

Tom gave him a finger cut across the throat to shut him up. Much more of this ad-libbing and the whole thing would fall apart.

"I have to go now. I hear them white devils coming for us. If I don't come back give my stuff to Cletus—", Jody cut the call in mid-sentence.

"We going to live, we going to live, praise God, Stinky, we going to live. That dumbass Jacques believed every word I say. Mr. Tom, Mr. Tiny, you got two good Yardies at your command," Jody said, dancing a jig around the cabin.

"Let's get our newest crew member below and tend to that shoulder before it gets infected, otherwise we'll have to cut it off," Tiny said, taking a close look at the festering wound.

The galley below decks served as the *Sea Bird's* sickbay when required and was stocked with a variety of medical instruments and medications that Tiny quickly laid out. A blanket was thrown on the mess table. Stinky laid down on his uninjured side, face scrunched up in pain, holding Tom's hand tightly. Without any hesitation, Tiny loaded up a syringe of morphine, plunged the needle into a vein on Stinky's arm, and pushed the plunger. In a few seconds the narcotic kicked in and Stinky drifted off to calypso land.

"You did that like an old junkie, Tiny," Tom said, as he flipped Stinky over on his stomach.

"Naw, Corpsman in the Navy. I was attached to a bunch of candy-assed jarheads that kept getting themselves shot so they could skate back in the rear for a few days of light duty. You never seen such crybabies in your life. Get a little gut shot, or a foot blown off, they scream like some teenage girl about to lose her cherry."

"Candy-assed Jarheads, huh? Skate duty, huh? Cherries, Huh? Tiny, if you didn't have that scalpel in your hand, I'd whoop your ass right here, right now, you fucking deck-ape," Tom said.

"Take it easy, Sarge. I said that just to get your attention. I'm going to cut this boy shoulder open and pull the barbed end out his back. I'll need you to help by sponging the blood so I can see inside to grab the barb. You up to it?"

"Gosh, Doc, *Blood*? I don't know man, what if I faint?" Tom said sarcastically.

"Okay then, here goes."

Without any hesitation, Tiny cut into Coco's back just below the shoulder blade at an upward angle, then proceeded with a smooth cut that ended at the armpit. Tom sopped up flowing blood as fast as he could, while Tiny stuck his fingers inside the incision hunting for the tip of the barbed bolt.

"Ouch! Found it."

Tiny quickly inserted a pair of surgical needle-nosed pliers, squeezed down on the barb tip, and pulled. In spite of the massive hit of morphine, Stinky let out a shout of pain. The barb was ripping flesh as it was being pulled through, blood was flowing a deep crimson. In the background, Jody was throwing up into a saucepan. Daisy was nowhere around.

One final steady pull and the bolt slid out. Tiny held it up for inspection, looking closely at the pieces of flesh stuck to the barbs. The barb blades alternated front to back attached to the bolt shaft. Any unlucky fish, or Yardie, shot with this would not be able to pull free from either direction. Cruel, but effective.

While Tiny was sewing Stinky up, Jody and Tom went topside to check the horizon for any nosey visitors, or danger. Tom nudged the throttle up a couple of notches, picked up the course of West-North-West, and put it on autopilot. Back on the fantail, Jody was wrapping Marcus in a piece of tarp, and then wrapped it with chain and cable to weight it down.

"Boss, Tom, I was just trying to think of something nice to say before we toss Marcus here out into the Blue, but you know what, there ain't anything nice to say. He's better off dead. His only future was being a Yardie all his life, just like the rest of us. Dead-end, no place to go, no future. We live in the most beautiful place in the world, but we've ruined it somehow. Look at me, I can't read or write. I don't know nothing about the world, nothing about my own people, nothing about life. I'm no better off than Marcus here. Sure makes a man think, don't it?"

"Jody, I think you're going to be fine. Most men go through life not knowing what it's all about, and then in the end they look back and say, 'Why, this is what I should have done,' or 'Why did I do that?' Just always try to do your best, that's all a man can do. If you fuck up, just suck it up and move on."

"Boss, nobody ever say that kind of stuff to me. I won't forget it. Now, let's toss this body over the side so he can rest in peace. Besides, I ain't never been to the Caymans"

CHAPTER 8

Jack's plane arrived an hour late causing him to miss his connecting flight to Tallahassee. The air turbulence over Cuba had been too much of a risk to fly through so the pilots had rerouted east and flew over Haiti then up to Miami. Once he debarked the jet, he bought a café con leche from a stand on the concourse, grabbed a seat in a waiting area, and called Bill Price.

"Marsh, I really don't want to talk to you just now. Can you call me back in a few years," Price said.

"Hi Billy, how's the wife and kids. I'm fine except for a bad case of the squirts."

"Knock it off, Marsh. I knew it was you. Caller I.D. If this is about Coco tell me, and then get off the line. Is she ok? Something happen to her?"

"No, Coco is fine, I guess. I haven't really talked to her in a few weeks."

"Yeah, I heard you're on the wagon. Is that right?"

"It's correct, I'm not sure about being right. Seriously, Bill, I can't give you an update on Coco. She's pretty upset with me. When was the last time you talked with her?"

"A couple of weeks. She's mad at me for not wanting to move to the Keys. She even told me she would give me half of her half ownership in the Sand Bar. I can't, Jack. I'm a cop, not a bartender."

"That's why I'm calling, Bill. I need to tell you about a situation I'm involved in. It's small now, but it's going to be a bitch if and when it becomes known." Jack sipped at the hot coffee.

There was a long silence. Jack blew on the hot brew, knowing what was coming.

"Marsh, you and I are not simpatico after the last small situation you had with the Haitian Tonton Macoute. Remember that one, or do I need to refresh your memory?"

"Not necessary, Bill. I remember it clearly. This is different."

Jack started at the beginning and told Captain Price everything that he knew about the Venezuelan submarine and its cargo. He didn't hold back about his suspicions regarding the potential trouble coming out of Houston and their plans to raise the wreck.

"Marsh, as usual you have understated the problem. Do you have any idea the kind of trouble coming your way? My advice is to back off and tell your Captain Burke to call the nearest Venezuelan consulate and turn it over to them. Anything short of that and you may find yourself dead, or worse, in some prison cell in one of those socialist worker paradise hell holes."

"Not me, Captain. I know when to duck and hide, and the more I think about what I could do with a billion bucks the less I'm afraid."

Another long silence. "You know I'll have to send this upstairs, Jack. If I know my boss, and I do, he'll beat feet over to the governor's mansion and get the weasel out of bed to tell him. And if I know the governor, and I do, then I wouldn't doubt for a second that he will think of a way to lay claim to your gold and confiscate it."

"Can't you sit on it for a while, Bill? I just wanted to give you a heads up in case something bad happens. Then you could ride to the rescue and earn another that-a-boy from a grateful state."

"Screw you. I'm trying to be realistic with you, Jack. I'm not sitting on it. In fact, since I am up to my ass here in the north end of the state, I'm thinking I'll send someone to tail you. Someone that will cuff you in a heartbeat the first time you break any laws."

"Swell. I call you for help, and you're sending a rent-a-cop to tail me."

"She's no rent-a-cop, buddy. You'll be sorry you ever ran across Agent Roberta Roberts if you fuck up. She's an ex-Feebie who got canned for taking too much initiative with some mutt in the Russian mafia. The mutt turns out to be a big donor to some sleaze-bag U.S. Senator and he drops a dime on her. I snatched her up the minute I heard she was cut loose."

"Great, just what I need, a woman cop tailing me. You're a real sweetheart, Billy. Remind me to tell Coco how helpful you are when a friend is in a bind."

"Fuck you, Marsh."

The phone went dead.

Chapter 9

Jack spent the night at the Miami Airport Hotel and picked up a rental car early the next morning. The drive down to Key West from Miami took a good couple of hours, most of it uneventful, which gave Jack time to pull a plan together that he felt comfortable with. All of the events over the last week had his mind whirling like a blender trying to make sense of the mix— Austin Burke and the gold discovery, two crewmembers who knew the location of the gold in Houston on R&R, another crewmember dead in Kingston, Burke's man Chandler sharing information with a Professor at Texas A&M. Tom and Jack show up at Burke's request, Burke wants Jack to use his contacts with the Florida Bureau of Investigation as a fallback plan. A lot of unconnected dots that needed connecting.

Burke, Tom, and Jack had all agreed about the potential danger of word getting out about the discovery, and the alarm that the news would create around the Islands. The decision to hold-close the discovery and tell only the minimum number of people about it was a good strategy, but now, Jack realized how impossible it was to keep it a secret. Too many people already knew about it. Meanwhile, Burke was in Houston meeting with his investors hoping to pull in enough cash to lease the lift boat in Louisiana, Tom was on the water with the *Sea Bird*, and he was in Key West craving a drink.

Jack was frustrated. He mentally broke the situation down into two categories; the first was to keep Burke, Tom and him out of danger. The second was to plan how they were going to get the gold up and back into the U.S. undetected. He started looking for weak spots. If trouble was going to come it would be from Burke's end. As soon as Burke met with his investors, it was going to be impossible to control events. Dick Chandler was in Houston and had probably met with his contact at the A&M campus in Galveston. Chandler's contact could then easily tell someone else about it, and that someone could be making plans of their own to recover the treasure. If Jack's assumptions were correct, Austin Burke needs to get his people and himself out of Houston and back on the *Sea Bird*.

The car lagging behind him had been on his tail since leaving the Hertz lot at Miami International. It was a dirty white with a dented fender. The driver was just a smudge of shadow in the rearview mirror, big and smudgy. Jack accelerated up to eighty, then backed off the gas pedal. The plain-wrap followed suit. It was either a cop or a bust. Local Miami thugs patrolled the isolated highway that ran from Key Largo to Key West preying on visitors, forcing them off the road, and robbing them at gunpoint. The gangbangers knew not to mess with a local out of fear that the local would shoot their ass in a heartbeat. The tourists caved without a struggle, handing over their vacation money, credit cards, and valuables. Jack hoped it was hijackers; he was in the mood for a little rumble. He did the hurry up and fall back routine a few more times, then ignored the car.

Jack punched up Austin Burke's cell number and hit his office number by mistake. He was punching off when the call was answered.

"Burke Explorations, this is Cara. How may I help you?"

"This is Jack Marsh calling for Austin Burke, please."

"I'm sorry Mr. Marsh, but Mr. Burke is not in today. Would you like to leave a message?"

"It's important that I talk with him immediately. It's in regards to Dick Chandler and his two men off the *Sea Bird*. I need to talk with him."

"Oh! Are you Austin's Marine friend?" Cara asked.

"That would be my friend, Tom Parker, but we're both working with Austin on his latest find."

"Oh, Mr. Marsh, I am so worried. I haven't heard a word from Mr. Burke since his meeting with the investors earlier today. I have tried reaching him everywhere, even the hospitals; there is no trace of him. Mr. Burke always stays in touch, even if he's out in the middle of the Gulf somewhere, he calls."

"Cara, are there other people in the office with you now?"

"Uh no, why? You're scaring me, Mr. Marsh"

"No, no, don't be afraid. I need you to do some things for me to help me find Austin, ok?"

"Sure, anything."

"When I was with Austin in Kingston, he said that two of his crew had left for a few days to be with their families. I need for you to contact them at their homes to check if they are ok."

"Sure, that would be Jim Taylor, and Sonny Powers. Jim lives in Pasadena, and Sonny lives over in Seabrook. I'll call them as soon as we finish here. Anything else?"

"Yeah, go through Austin's computer, and load a flash drive of all the data he may have on his current expedition. Give me everything, names of his investors he met with today, banker, survey plans, expedition findings, anything unusual. I need to know if he has talked to or contacted by any Caribbean any government officials, or permitting departments, things like that. I want a list of his competitors too. Anyone who would want to see Austin in trouble, or pushed to the side."

"Wow! That's a lot. How fast do you need all this?"

"I'll give you an hour to pull together what you can. The sooner I know what he has done and who he has talked with the sooner I can track him down," he said. They exchanged cell numbers and emails. By the time he hit Key West she should have some of it.

Jack was blowing over the Seven Mile Bridge, south of Marathon in the Middle Keys at seventy-five, all the windows were down, XM radio was set on a Chicago Blues station. Big Mama Thornton was wailing on her harmonica. Jack pounded the dash to the beat. The crystal green and blue waters that flashed by on either side were like a giant flawed uncut diamond, held up to the sun, its rays reflecting a galaxy of never before seen colors. A formation of cruising pelicans flew across the bridge, lazily pumping their wings in lock step, (or is it lock-wing?) trying to find a current of air they could hook on for a free ride. The trade winds blowing out of the southeast were pushing a dark bank of heavy thunderclouds up from Cuba, aimed for the Keys.

He just dropped down off the bridge onto Bahia Honda Key when his cell rang. He pulled over onto a crushed coral turn-out, shaded in coconut palms, and grabbed the phone,

"Marsh."

"Mr. Marsh, this is Cara. I thought I better call you about Jim Taylor and Sonny Powers, the two deck hands on the *Sea Bird*."

"What did you find?" he asked.

"Well, I talked with Jim's wife. She told me that Jim is home, and has been drinking a lot, which is not unusual when he's home. Mrs. Taylor said that Jim had been talking crazy about them coming into some big money real soon, once Mr. Burke gets some front money to bring up an enemy submarine loaded with gold."

"Doesn't sound like any problem there, as long he is home drinking and not out in a bar somewhere," Jack said.

"Yeah, you're probably right, but then Mrs. Taylor told me about what she heard a couple of days ago when Sonny Powers came by to talk with Jim. Sonny said that an old friend of his from Huntsville, a guy called Mad Mike, wanted him to join in on a job that would bring in fifty thousand dollars each when it was finished. It would only take a few days down in Key West to do the job. Sonny wanted Jim to go with him, but he turned him down, saying he was sticking close to home in case Mr. Burke calls him back out. At that, Sonny just laughed, and said something about, "He'll be waiting a long time." Cara stopped to catch her breath, "Well, it turns out that after Sonny left, Jim told her that Sonny was an ex-con, and any friend from

Huntsville was probably another ex-con scheming on some kind of hit, or something illegal."

"When did Mrs. Taylor say this conversation between Sonny and Jim took place?"

"Yesterday."

As Jack sat digesting this latest twist in events, he watched the plain-wrap coming off the bridge and pull in next to him under the palms. The driver sat looking across at him, wearing aviator type sunglasses, and chewing on a toothpick.

"Ok, Cara, email me a photo of Sonny Powers, if you have one, and a copy of his employment application. After you get all the info I asked for, lock up the place, and go home. I'll get back in touch with you the minute I hear from Austin, or with any other news. You got all that?"

"Yes, I'll be out of here in no time. I have everything backed up on my laptop so I can work from home. Mr. Marsh, please keep me updated. I am really worried about what may be going on."

"I promise, Cara," he said, and hung up.

Jack got out of his rental car and leaned into the plain-wrap.

"Let me guess, you want my money and watch or you'll shoot me," he said.

"Sir, do you realize that you were doing seventy-five in a forty-five speed zone? I could have you arrested for reckless driving. Instead I think I'll just *bitch-slap* you for forcing me to keep up with you in this piece of crap death trap."

"Ouch! Strong language coming from a ... lady. You must be Agent Roberts of the Florida Bureau of Investigation. Am I right?" he asked, straight faced.

"Cut the crap, Marsh. Captain Price told me to hang onto you like a tick on a dog. He said you're in deep doodoo and that I should let you sink, but not let you drown."

"Yep, deep doodoo! That's what I was telling Price a few hours ago. Now fast-forward a couple of hours, and things are a lot worse,"

Bobbie held up her hands as if to ward off his sarcasm, "Sit tight, I'm calling Price and you can tell him directly about what's happened since you two turds talked," she said and hit the speed dial on a small chunky gadget, and was on instantly

Captain Price answered immediately. "Talk to me, Marsh. I'm tired, busy, and feel like killing something, so none of your jeez, life is good crap."

Bobbie placed the gadget on the dashboard, speaker facing me.

"Billy, how about you cutting the crap and start taking me serious? I'm sitting on a powder keg and the fuse is getting shorter by the hour.

"Jack, I have a pissed-off boss on my hands because of you and your powder keg. He went to the governor with your story and the governor gave him a direct order that any bullion brought in to Florida by you will be confiscated as state property. Furthermore, if you and your buddies are caught and held in some offshore jail cell we are to deny any knowledge. You understand all that?" He paused to let that sink in and to take a deep breath.

"Now, as a friend, I'll tell you what I said earlier…cease and desist. You're only going to get yourself in trouble. Knowing you the way I do though, I know you will proceed as you damn well please. I have given Agent Roberts an order to not let you out of her sight. She is to stick to you like glue, even if she has to cuff herself to you, she is to keep you alive and out of trouble. You do as she says or I swear I'll have her snap your skinny neck. Now tell me what's transpired since we talked last night."

"Whoa, Bill. This is no way to treat a friend. I confided in you, brought you in on the biggest discovery since the *Ottacha* treasure. Now, you're trying to slow me down with Godzilla here…"

"Hold on slick, you referring to me as Godzilla? If you have any hopes of ever having kids, you better take that back or I'll crush those puny nuts of yours into peanut butter," Bobbie said, as she clenched her fists open and closed.

Jack looked at her big hands, then looked in her eyes. A chill pierced his chest.

"Hey, just a figure of speech, ok?" he said, then focused back on the speaker box. "If you want to know what I know, then we're going to have to be civil. You don't want to piss me off. I have my pistol pointing at Agent Robert's pea-brain, as we speak. One more threat, and she's going to be missing the part that holds her ABC's. Now let's start over."

"Dammit, Jack, you know what I mean. Do we have to go through this every time we talk? You know we're on your side on this thing, so damnit, cut it out, and let's get to work. Tell me what you know…. please."

Five minutes later, the only sound was of the wind blowing through the car windows. Agent Roberts sat quietly clenching her fists, making her knuckles pop, working her toothpick from side to side. Price was quietly digesting everything. The only sound was the galactic squabbling from the speaker

"Well?" Jack asked.

"Well, what?" Price answered.

"I don't know. You're the cop, what do we do next?"

"Dammit Marsh, give me a few minutes to digest all this."

"While you're digesting, I'll tell you my next steps. First thing is to find Burke and his man, Chandler. I have a creepy feeling that someone else is in the game. I don't know who, but Burke wouldn't just drop off the radar without sending up a flare."

Jack was worried. He didn't like unknowns, and he didn't believe in coincidences. "I know one of his crew is home drunk. The other one may be on his way to find me with some ex-con named Mad Mike. Second, I'm going to call Tom Parker on the *Sea Bird*, and bring him up to date. Then I'm going home, clean my Glock, put some claymores out, and set up an ambush for Mr. Sonny Powers and Mad Mike. If and when they come sniffing around, I'll be waiting. If they don't show after a few days, then I'll chalk it up to nerves and head back to Jamaica."

"Marsh, if you go down there, I won't be able to cover you. I don't have any jurisdiction; you'll be on your own."

"I'm a big boy, Bill, I'm pretty good at staying alive… most of the time. I don't want you to put your job on the line over this. I think I'm just jumpy over not knowing who all the players are, and where they are."

"Let's do this. You make your calls, get everyone in a safe place, then pack your bags. Meanwhile, I'll get some eyes on Houston and put out an APB on Burke. I'll also pull up everything we can find on this Sonny Powers and his friend, Mad Mike whatever. I don't want you ducking out for Jamaica until we talk, OK?"

"OK."

"OK, get going. Bobby, stick with Jack for now. I'll keep you updated as things are known." The gadget went dead.

"The ABC part of my brain? Cute, Marsh, real cute," Bobby said, as she tucked away the communication device.

Chapter 10

Pulling into Key West, Jack checked to make sure Bobbie was behind him as he turned onto North Roosevelt. The wind had picked up and dark thunderclouds were rolling in. At Eaton, he took a right, crossed over the charter boat slips, then passed the Navy base housing area, and pulled in the parking lot in front of the Raw Bar.

His plan was to go by foot from the Raw Bar to his place a few blocks over. He wasn't taking any chances, knowing that there were possibly two gunslingers in town waiting to drop him, maybe more.

Jack pulled Bobbie into the Turtle Kraals gift shop and told her to lose the white short-sleeved button-down shirt and the black skinny tie.

"Hey, screw you, Marsh. Somebody doesn't like the way I dress, I'll bust their gonads."

"Agent Roberts, if you're going to hang with me, you must get out of that Blues Brothers clown suit."

While he waited, he punched in Claire's number, and got her recording again. He hung up, and kicked a cloud of coral dust out of frustration. This was the third call since he had arrived back in Florida and was really getting worried about her. He called Donnie's B&B number, and got his answering machine. 0 for 2.

He flipped the phone closed, and turned to see what was keeping Bobbie,

"Bobbie? Is that you?" he asked, not quite believing his eyes. The Blues Brother's outfit was gone, evidently in the canvas bag under her arm. Jack was speechless. She clashed with nature, tie-died t-shirt under a bright fluorescent green shirt with a coconut and tiki print, camouflaged cargo shorts with huge side pockets, red flip flops, and a I ♥ Key West cap. *Whew!*

"Of course it's me! Who were you expecting? You told me to blend in. Well I'm blending, Dickhead."

"Why I... think you are tricked out perfectly. The locals will think you're on the lam, and the tourists will think you're a local," he said, nodding his head approvingly.

"Thanks, Jack, I needed a compliment about now after being laughed at by that walking tattoo behind the counter. He lost the humor when I pointed my Nine at him and flashed the shield," she grinned.

They started out on foot, ignoring the sniggers from a group of tourists as they passed. Miss Key West wanted to stop and kick some butt, but Jack pulled her away before she threw a roundhouse. They split up when they crossed Elizabeth Street. Jack sent Bobbie down to the corner of his alley as he hustled around the block to the other end. The sketchy plan was to approach his house from both ends, looking for any one that didn't fit in.

A half block from the alley, his cell phone rang.

"Marsh," he answered.

"Jack, its Claire...."

"Claire, thank God! I have been worried to death about you. Where are you?"

"You're so sweet. I haven't had anyone worry about me for a long time. Come on home and I'll cook you my lasagna specialty."

"You're at your house?" he asked. "How long have you been there?"

"I just walked in and listened to your messages. I pulled a three-shifter at the Base sickbay. A couple of the regular M.D.'s were called out with the Coasties on something. Then we had to transfer a gun wound patient up to the Miami V.A. Hospital, and I was there the rest of the night. Stupid me, I left my cell phone at the clinic during the rush to get the patient to Miami."

"Is everything ok? I mean, is your place in order, no visitors, or break-ins?"

"No, why? What's going on, Jack?"

"Stay in your house, lock the doors. I'll be there in three minutes."

It took less than a minute to reach the alley off Emma Street. He took a few deep breaths and then eased in behind a clump of large philodendron plants to get a look for anything out of place. The alley's surface was made from crushed coral mixed with dirt-filled potholes deep enough to ruin your day. Dead palm fronds camouflaged the water-filled holes that could cause mental havoc to the old homeless 'Nam vets who cruised the back alleys keeping a wary eye out for trip wires and punji pits. Most of the backyard fences along the alley leaned at angles by the weight of the bougainvillea, tropical flower shrubs, and clusters of banana palms heavy with growing fruit. The triple canopy overhead kept the alley shadowed and cool through the hot and humid days year round. Huge gumbo-limbo trees, Malaysian coconut palms, and ancient banyans cast shadows that never stopped shifting, Jack was a little spooked himself when walking the alley at night.

Jack spotted Bobbie at the other end of the alley and signaled for her to stay put while he peeped up close. He watched as she faded into the foliage, then moved up slowly, hugging the fence line, keeping a wary eye on the trees overhead. The fence that ran in front of his place was kept freshly painted and in good repair. Except for all the dog crap from Donnie's sissy Pitbull, Petunia, the coral road was clean. He squatted, peering into the yard. Claire's little house was closest to the alley, while his sat back deeper in the yard. He hopped over the fence and made it up to Claire's porch.

"Jack," Claire whispered through her latched screen door, "I think there's someone in your place. Come here," she said, opening her screen.

From her bedroom window, he scanned left to right, focusing on the front windows and door. He saw a shadow flit by one of the windows and quickly disappear back into the gloom. The hackles on his neck stood out in alarm.

"Claire, what kind of weapon do you keep?"

"A weapon? Let's call the police."

"No, not yet. There is a state agent outside already. Now, what do you have I can use for a few minutes?"

Claire went over to her nightstand, pulled out a small .38 automatic, ratcheted back the slide, chambering a round like a pro, and handed it to him

"It shoots high, and right," she said.

"Thanks, sweetheart," he said in his best Bogart voice. "Now, you stay here, keep down below the window sills, and don't come out until I call for you."

He eased out her back door and walked carefully up to his porch, keeping to the blind side of the windows. He heard someone talking excitedly inside, and then realized it was the TV. He heard a laugh that sounded like it came from the couch in the right hand corner.

Jack caught movement out of the corner of his eye and spotted Bobbie hugging the sidewall of Donnie's B&B upfront. He signaled her that there was at least one person inside and to come forward. Bobbie looked like a panther stalking its prey as she approached the porch in a running crouch, pistol up and ready, eyes bright with adrenaline. Jack slowly turned the doorknob, gave Bobbie the nod, and threw the door open. Bobbie was inside in a nanosecond,

"FREEZE! STATE POLICE! On the floor. On the floor, Asshole!" Bobbie's shouted commands reverberated up and down the alley.

"I ain't done it. I swear I ain't done it. Please don't shoot." A terrified Tyrone Caldwell wailed as he threw himself on the floor with his big hands covering his ears, and rolled up in a fetal position.

"Tyrone? What the fuck are you doing in my house?" Jack said.

He swept the living room, then kicked the bedroom door open. There was a body hog-tied with rope and duct tape lying on the bed, *'The fuck?'*

"What the hell is going on here?" he demanded, as he stood in the doorway watching the body and Tyrone at the same time. He glanced over to the front door. Claire was standing there with a hand over her mouth, wide eyed.

"I can 'splain it, Mr. Marsh, I can, yes indeedy, I can. Just please don't shoot me. I done been shot once before. It missed, but I could feel it in my brain, jess like it hit me."

"Ok, ok, take it easy, Tyrone. Get up on the couch."

"Hey, Ace, let me cuff him until we know the story around here," Bobbie said.

"I don't think we need to worry about Tyrone. He's a friend."

"Yes, Sir, that's exactly right. Me and Mr. Marsh is friends. I'm his personal counselor on things," Tyrone said with pride.

"Personal counselor? What kind of things?"

"Things. Shine'n things."

"Excuse me," Bobbie said, signaling she wanted more information.

"I'll explain later. Let's hear what he has to say," Jack said. "OK, Tyrone, from the top."

"Yes Sir. Mama Dey tell me to keep looking out over here while you away. She says something big happening out in the Islands and you caught up in it. She says she getting messages from over there about something going amok, big trouble on the way, and you in the middle." Tyrone wiped his sweaty face with a big blue hanky, then stuffed it back in his pocket.

"So I come over here and hang out looking and waiting for trouble. Well, sure enough, she come along a couple of nights ago. I was sitting across the alley up in that big gumbo-limbo tree and I sees something moving inside your place here. I near fell out of that tree I so scared. I didn't feel nothing at first, but then I started to get them vibrations that something really bad was inside your place. My head started seeing red and it kept getting redder and redder. I just squished my eyes tight not even looking over there. I sat up in that tree for I don't know how long, until the red started to go away. I stayed there another hour. I got my nerve up and climbed down from the tree, and come over to your house. Goose bumps running up and down my arms and back like they's in a 'tater race. I couldn't feel anybody inside so I opened up the door and let myself in. Sometimes I don't need no light to see things. So I just stood there a looking and a reaching out. I tippy-toed over to right where you is standing and I could feel something scary in that bedroom. I peeked inside and almost poo myself. There on the bed was that." He pointed to the kitchen table.

A glass jar with a lid on it sat on the table, inside was a little bundle of feathers wrapped with a piece of cloth. Jack went over to it and started to pick it up....

"Don't you touch that," Tyrone yelled. "You touch it, you dead. Come away from that thing." Tyrone motioned him away. "That the worse thing in the world. Nobody do that no more, onliest the really bad river people."

"What is it?" Bobbie asked, looking at it from her position by the door, not daring to get closer.

"It a juju that give you the blood fever. You get it and you boil inside until you dead," Tyrone said not taking his eyes off the sealed jar.

"A juju? You mean voodoo juju, a fetish of some sort?" Bobbie asked.

"Some folks might call it a voodoo, or a hoodoo, or a doodoo, don't matter, it all the same. It'll take you down, even if you alive or if you dead. Ain't no medicine can touch it. When I see that thing lying on your bed Jack, I ran to Mama Dey as fast as my feet would fly. She come over here in her nightie, takes one look at that thing, chased me out, ran home herself, and got that jar. She came back here, saying her prayers and a singing, soon as that evil spirit go to sleep she snatched it up and stuffed it inside that jar. Just like that," he said, as he snapped his fingers. "Me and her went home and took turns climbing in that rain barrel to wash that demon off. That the only thing that protect you, old rain water been a sitt'n for a while."

They stood staring at the jar for a few minutes. The prickly hair on Jack's neck was back. Bobby rolled her toothpick around with a sneer on her face.

"What about the 911 in the bedroom? How did he die?" Bobbi asked, not taking her eyes off the jar.

"Die? He ain't dead, he's sleeping. I been giving him some of Mama's smelling drops every few hours. He been sleeping all along. Now, his friend might be dead, I don't know."

"What friend? Start at the top, Tyrone, tell us everything," Jack said.

"I come back to your place here about three in the morning after I take my rainwater bath. Well, I come up on the porch and the door swung open and that man in there jump out with a gun in his hands. It happened so quick, I thinking it some woo-hoo coming after me, so I slap that gun out my face and screamed like a little girl. Well, I guess I must a hit that man extra hard because he fell back into the living room here and hit his head on the coffee table. That gun went off, *KABOOM!* like a lightning bolt. This whole room lit up, and in the flash I see this other man a holding his stomach, face all scrunched up in pain. I turned around, jumped that fence like it was a foot high, and went and hid in Mr. Donnie's front bushes. About ten minutes later, I see this man bending over holding his gut come staggering out of the alley. I give it another few minutes and come back in here. I see that one still snoozing, so I trundled him up really good and been sitting here waiting for you to come home and give you the report." Tyrone finished up, as he looked around the room at each one of us.

The room was silent, as we all looked at Tyrone, then the bedroom door, then the sealed jar.

"Ok, folks, I'm declaring this a police crime scene, everybody up and out. Don't touch anything. Watch where you step," she said.

She motioned to Tyrone, "On your feet big guy, hands behind your back," she said, and cuffed him. "I said outside, everybody, now move!"

Twenty minutes later, there was pandemonium. The alley was jammed with County and City units, emergency lights twirling. City cops were running crime scene tape and barricades across both ends of the alley. The paramedics appeared a few minutes later and hustled inside, then hurried out with the unconscious man strapped on a litter. Ten minutes after that the entire backyard was closed down. The fire department's Haz-Mat crew were suited up and covering the small house in plastic sheets. The jar with the fetish in it was placed in a lead-lined container and whisked away. Donnie's partner, Duncan, was in hysterics, and given a sedative by a sympathetic B&B guest.

CHAPTER 11

Claymore-sized pellets of rain shot down in slanted sheets hitting Symington Street's molten asphalt, mimicking big drops of super-heated wok grease vaporizing before they could puddle. The combination of heat and humidity formed a wall that closed in on Jack that triggered a half-dozen phobias. Sweat ran down his chest and back causing his shirt to cling to him like a junkie clings to his dime bag. Jack's mood was as black as a pimp's heart. Things were not going his way. When that happened, he got pissy with the people around him, said things he didn't mean, picked fights…in the old days he would have a couple of belts of firewater and hit somebody with a pool stick, '*Avenge the Red Man.*'

"What?" he said, turning to Claire.

"Jack, stop with the brooding. That's not going to solve anything. Finish eating and try to relax."

They were sitting in the Raw Bar, his second favorite place to eat after the Sand Bar. The Raw Bar was built out over the water near the boat docks and was popular with the locals. They were sharing a fried grouper sandwich and a cup of conch chowder. Rain hitting the tin roof sounded like strings of firecrackers at a Chinese funeral. Lightning slashed out, silhouetting boats anchored out in the harbor, followed by bunker-buster explosions of thunder. The perfect night for a murder.

"Yeah, I know, but sometimes I just want to punch something," he said, and then quickly thought how juvenile that sounded. What happened to his self-motivational ass-kicker front, '*Suck it up*, Take *the pain*,' and '*Come out shooting*,' or his all-time favorite, '*Whoever eats the fastest, gets the mostest*'? He laughed and the gloom lifted.

"Christ, I've really mucked this one up. We're homeless, Tyrone's in jail, Sonny Powers is in isolation, and Donnie is threatening to sue me for creating unwanted attention to his B&B. The other hit man is in the wind, and some witch doctor wants to kill me," he said, as he ticked off each point on his fingers. "On top of that, Bobbie has gone postal with all this State Agent crap. She's got the Monroe County Sheriff and his deputies ready to lay on a couple of knuckle sandwiches the first chance they get her alone. To top it off, she's doubling down by calling in a crew of Miami agents."

They caught each other's eyes and smiled. Grins that turned to laughter began to spread and they just let it roll. Laughter was like one of Mama Dey's elixirs, and they rode it out, wiping their eyes with paper napkins.

"If this is what life is going to be like with you, Marine, then count me in," Claire said, eyes twinkling.

"Yeah, tell me that in a couple of weeks," Jack said. "Claire, I'm serious. if you're smart you'll get up, pay the check, and run as fast as you can. Don't look back until you hit Disney World. Hook up with Goofy, or one of the Dwarfs, anybody but me."

"Oh Jack, you're being silly. Cut it out. You know you need me. Once this is behind us, things will be fine. Right now, it's just so overwhelming. For example, where do we sleep tonight, what are we going to wear tomorrow, what about my job? Everything I own is in that house and God only knows when they'll let me back in. Same with your place.

"That stuff is minor. Let's finish up then we'll go over to the Hilton and get a suite. Later, we can hit some shops on Duval and pick up whatever we need. The big question is what I do about the mutt on the loose and the juju man?" he said, as he answered the vibrating cell phone.

"Yeah?" he said.

"Jack, this is Bobbie. I'm glad I caught you. Things are starting to go from bad to worse. Sonny Powers is talking like a canary on speed. We can't shut the man up. His partner is named Michael Burr, goes by Mad Mike. He and Sonny did time together in Huntsville. They were down here to pop you, and then go back to Houston. He was supposed to collect fifty large for doing you, then another fifty for Austin Burke. He said that they had Burke in a motel ready to do the deed. Somehow, Burke broke loose, crashed through the front plate glass window, and ran off."

"You've been a busy girl, Bobbie."

"That's only half of it, Ace. Seems like Sonny has some kind of virus or something. His body is breaking out in a rash and his temperature hit one-oh-four a little while ago. They are transferring him over to the Navy Base in a little while and put him in quarantine until they figure out what he's got. Meanwhile, a couple of deputies are talking with Tyrone to find out more on this blood-fever sickness he told us about, then they'll cut him loose. There's nothing they can hold him on. I had the Haz-Mat people run the jar with the thing-a-mabob in it up to the University of Miami Med School to let them see what's inside."

"Damn, Bobbie, where is this going?" he said out of frustration.

"That's the good news. Seems like your buddy Mad Mike checked himself into the local V.A. clinic the other night with a gunshot wound to the abdomen, and was transferred up to the Miami V.A. to be sewn up..."

"Hold it for a second," Jack said, turning to Claire. "What was the name of the guy you took to Miami? The one with the gunshot wound."

"Oh uh, Michael something-or-other. Michael Brown... Bro—

"Burr?" he asked.

"Yes, that was it, Burr, Mike Burr."

"Bobbie, did you hear that?"

"Yeah Ace, I heard it, don't matter though. Mad Mike slipped away from the ward he was in and has disappeared."

"What do you mean *disappeared*?"

"Disappeared, as in gone, vanished, ok."

"Crap! This guy could be on his way down here to finish the job,"

Jack scanned the other tables. The place was crowded with tourists and locals sitting shoulder to shoulder eating and enjoying themselves.

"Listen, Bobbie, I don't like this at all. Key West is a small town, and it wouldn't take much for this guy to track me down. I think I'm going to skip out on you for the duration."

"Uh-uh, no deal. You aren't going anywhere. Captain Price will be down here in the wee hours. He specifically told me to sit on you until he gets here. There's a part I left out, Ace, our man Sonny Powers also told us that he and Mad Mike were given the go-ahead to pop Tiny Miles and Tom Parker as part of the Austin contract you and Burke were on. Price said he also wants clarification from you on who else might be privy to the location of the site."

"Clarification? I told him everything I know. There isn't anything else to tell. I'm out of here. I'm dropping off the grid."

"Ain't going to work, Ace. I want you and Claire to get a couple of rooms somewhere, and sit tight until you hear from me. OK?"

"I swear, Bobbie, after this, me and Price are finished. You tell him that for me. We'll be at the Hilton on Mallory Square. How about you, you want me to get you a room?"

"Nah, my per-diem doesn't fit; I'll crash around the office here somewhere."

"Bullshit, I'll get you a room. You and Price can practice full nelsons, or something," he smiled, and hung up.

"Let's get out of here. I want to make a stop before we go to the hotel. Maybe pick up some shaving gear and whatever girls need," he said, helping Claire up from her chair.

By the time they got across the lot to the rental car they were soaked. Before they made their dash, a local told them the storm would be hanging over the lower Keys for a couple of days.

'*Maybe that'll keep all the tourists up north, give us a break from the fucking gawkers,"* he had monotoned in a *boozy baritone.*

Jack found Mama Dey's place off the alley behind Emma Street in Old Town, and parked a few doors down. Before getting out, he checked the pistol he had grabbed from his closet before being chased out by the Haz-mat people. It was a worn Walther PPK 9mm that he had bought years before from a man who needed a few bucks to get out of the Keys. There wasn't a serial number or factory marking anywhere on the piece. The magazine held ten rounds with one in the chamber. In spite of its age it didn't rattle and was nice and tight, just the way 007 liked his.

The alley was dark and filled with moving shadows as the wind-whipped rain beat against them. A sharp lance of lightning bounced across the sky as they stepped up on the small porch, the boom of thunder masked his knock. He was about to knock again when the door opened and Mama Dey motioned them in.

"I was expecting you, Jack, and I'm glad you brought Miss Claire. I sent for you as soon as I got the news," Mama Dey said, as she sat in a wooden straight-backed chair.

Jack had never noticed how small she was until just now. Her bare feet didn't touch the ground even though she was perched on the edge of the chair. Her long grey hair was in a braid over her shoulder. Through a trick of the lantern glow he couldn't tell her age. It was like one of those kids' toys with the special lens that when held one-way it showed one thing, held another direction and it was something else. One moment she was old, the next.... He looked away.

"You sent for me?" he questioned.

"Why yes Jack, I did send for you, child," she smiled.

Jack didn't *even* want to go there.

"Well then, I'm here. What's the news?" he said as if he had received her hoodoo-gram, and rushed right over.

"Jack, you need to go to Jamaica, and stop the *Kakwa Nkisi*. She cut loose the Baboon from his sleep, now we all scared what's going to happen. That Jacques Lapin jackal on the loose too. He needs to be stopped, he's planning on using the blood sickness to steal the treasure."

"Mama, I don't have a clue of what you are saying. Can you say it in plain words?"

"In the old village, there is a river that runs through it where the people get their water. It is the cleanest water in the whole Congo, and all the animals come and drink from it. In the old times, a family of baboons moved in close to the Bakongo people. The baboons would steal food at night from the village, sometimes they'd grab a baby or small child from the village, take it off and kill it. Later on, when the village people found the dead child, anyone who touched that child's body got the blood fever and died. All the *Nkisi,* medicine men would cast spells on the baboons and everything would quiet down for a while. Then pretty soon, the baboons would visit the village and here comes that blood fever again and more of our people would die. So the tribe moved the village farther down river and life would go back to normal. Onetime, some young boys killed a baboon on a hunting trip and ate it. Well, all them boys died. Since that time, the *Nganga Nkisi,* evil medicine men, use baboon blood when they want someone to die. They soak it in a juju, and when that person touches it he will die."

"Where is this village, Mama Dey?" Claire asked as if anticipating the answer.

"The Kikwit village, where the Ebola River runs into the Congo River, close to old Zaire...."

"Oh my God! You're talking about Ebola! Blood fever. Now it makes sense. The Zaire Ebola virus, the deadliest form of Ebola there is. Mortality rate is almost ninety percent, Jack. That thing in your bedroom had the Ebola virus. That's what Sonny Powers has. Oh my God! I've got to let the clinic know immediately, anyone who came in contact with that thing has to be checked out."

"We didn't touch it. It was in that jar," Jack said, checking his hands for some sign of something.

"The virus can only spread by contact with an infected person, body fluids, blood, person to person, sneezing, mucus, eating after an infected person. Incubation period is two to ten days and starts out as a rash and high fever. It's one of the most painful deaths there is. You bleed to death inside, as the virus eats through your organs and tissue from the inside out, eventually breaking out in little bloody puncture wounds all over your body," Claire explained.

"How do you know about Jacques Lapin, and the uh… treasure?" Jack said.

"Same way I know that gorilla woman that follows you around is standing out there in the rain, under that big gumbo tree. Go tell her to sit up on the porch before she catches something," she said, shaking her head. "Lawdy, Lawdy, suffer the chilrun."

Jack went out on the porch and yelled for Bobbie.

"Over here, Ace," she said, stepping out from behind a huge tree, dripping wet.

"Come up on the porch, and get out of the rain," he said, shaking his head in wonderment. He went back inside.

There were a million questions running through his mind. Were Claire and he exposed to the virus? How does Mama Dey know all this, and where does she get all her information? Where was Mad Mike Burr? Who's behind the contract on Burke and everyone associated with him? Is Tom safe?

"Jack, you ain't got time to be worried about all those things," Mama Dey said, pointing a gnarled knuckled finger at him.

"We got to get going tonight. We got fixens to pull together. I got to get my bag ready. Don't let me forget that quart a conch chowder in the ice box, Oola never forgive me... and send that gorilla woman to pick up Tyrone. He's walking home in the rain over on Truman Street," she went on as she bustled around the small room.

"Mama, hold on. Where are *we* going? What is it that *we* are going to do?" Jack asked, knowing he wasn't going to like the answer.

"Jack, you going to Jamaica with me and Tyrone. You going to rent one of them airplanes out at the airport, and we going to fly. Sister Oola going to meet us with a ride, then we going to trap us a hyena and its whelp."

Claire and Jack looked at each other, at a complete loss of comprehension.

"Slow down, Mrs. Dey. We aren't going anywhere until we know what the hell it is that you are talking about," Jack said harshly.

"You listen to me, Whitey Mon. You be talking to Mama Dey. You know what Dey means? No, of course you don't. Dey means *Guardian*. We the guardian of the

Family's Spirits for all times. We *Bakongo Nganga,* Holy People. We been tending the Family since before the waters come, since before the Lamb taken to Golgotha, before Muhammad claim the throne. We from the original Family of the land, even before time official and there ain't no clocks, we be here. People from every village in the land come to us to look on the other side to see what's coming, and what's going. We be forever. We be generation after generation of guardians. With that burden, we be given the Sight of Spirits. We be able to see and hear things normal folks can't. We got to fight evil with evil. They's only a few of us left and evil's starting to win. We got to kill him wherever we find him. If I say go, we go. I'm the Guardian Mother, Jack. My people needs me, and I needs you to get me there. I saved you from the Monkey, now you going to save me from the Jackal. That's all there is to that."

Claire and Jack decided that she would take the rental to get her to the base hospital and get the word out on the Ebola virus. Her biggest concern was that if it spread, they could have a major pandemic on their hands. The only known cure is containment at the source, and then let it run its course.

She gave Jack a kiss and a tight hug.

"Don't get hurt, Marine. I'm not going to be there to kiss it and make it better," she said, kissing him again, and then she was gone.

While Bobbie went to find Tyrone, Jack called information for a private flight service. He knew that the small executive jet services were hungry for business trying to cover their monthly nut plus overhead.

The first place he called, the phone was answered before the ring ended,

"Executive Flights, Mel speaking," an alert chipper voice answered in spite of the late hour.

"Do you have something that can make it down to Kingston, four passengers, traveling light?"

"Yes sir, I sure do. I have a Beech Premier sitting on the tarmac as we speak. She's gassed, and she's fast," Mel said.

"Spool her up, I'll be out there in an hour, ready to go."

"But I haven't told you the cost, or about the meal service, beverages...."

"Mel, the deal is closed, stop selling. Give me whatever service is standard. Hold off on the booze and load up on sandwiches and fruit juices." Jack gave Mel a credit card number and hung up.

CHAPTER 12

Key West was saturated from the tropical depression dumping water over the region. Jack was on foot, walking from Mama Dey's place over to his. His shoes and socks were soaked, shirt and pants clinging to his skin. He held himself tight from the chill. The night was slick and cobalt-black filled with shadows whipped around from the gusty wind and saltwater-laced rain. Streetlamps scattered shards of light off pooled water, triggering his eyes to snap to the movement looking for danger. The yellow crime-scene tape across the alley entrance fluttered like a kite's tail in the wind. Rain drops bounced off the elephant ears and banana leaves popping like cap guns in a kid's shoot out, causing him to flinch with each imaginary volley.

His plan was simple. Look for Mad Mike Burr by backtracking to the scene of the crime. When he found him, well, he would think about that when it happened. After telling Bill Price everything about the gold, he felt like a weight had been lifted off of him. Now, he could focus on what he should have been doing since Dick Chandler and Austin Burke disappeared. He had lost his edge by trying to cover every one's ass by being a good citizen. That wasn't him. There was gold out there waiting. Billions of dollars of it. What the fuck was wrong with him? He needed to get back out on the Blue and bring that gold up into the light of day. He was beginning to get a little confidence back then the vision of the feathered juju hit him. What was with all the hocus-pocus voodoo crap? You smoke enough of that island ganja and you can see just about anything you want to see. *'Sorry, not this Surfer Dude.'*

Mama Dey threw a fit when he told her he wasn't going with her and Tyrone to Jamaica. Once she explained that he needed to find the man trying to kill him and the people around him, she calmed down a bit. He reasoned with her that his finding these people was just as important to all of their safety as it was for her to kill the Jackal.

"Jack, what you say is right. You got to get that man before he kills you. Me and Sister Oola can handle that fat buffalo down there on top of that mountain. Besides, I got me a secret weapon ain't nobody knows about," she said as she pointed to Tyrone. "This boy just vibrating with energy. I get him to stop picking his nose long enough to get him on the other side, he's going to be leading an army of spirit warriors. They be lined up shoulder to shoulder all the way from yesterday into tomorrow, beating their shields with them spears. Just like the Elders say, going to sound like a million zebras racing across the parched earth with the smell of water in their nostrils, except it going to be the Lamb chasing the Baboon back to the river."

Jack looked at Tyrone as Mama was talking and caught him discreetly pulling his hand away from his face.

"What? I ain't done nothing. I's ready to make the jump, Mama, anytime you say," he said defensively.

Mama Dey shook her head, as if in doubt, "Jack, you did your part, you got me a ride down there. You go do what you going to do, then get yourself out of these here Islands. You're too easy a target, and I can't be protecting you all the time," she said as she rummaged around an old cigar box,

"Here, you keep this close to you, and you'll be safe," she said as she handed him a dime-sized ball of old hair with colored thread laced through it.

"What is it?" he asked, as he rolled it around in his palm.

"It's a grain of sand from the Old Village. I'm not saying the old village by the Ebola River. I'm saying the *original* Old Village, the one where the laws were laid down. That grain of sand's as old as time Jack, and there ain't nothing more precious than time. You carry that like Mama say and you a part of that time. You be blessed son, now git. I got to pack a few more things before I go wrestle with that Hyena."

Jack cut through Donnie's side yard to get as close to his place as he could without being seen by anyone on watch. He ducked behind a huge elephant ear plant, squinting into the shadows. He detected movement ahead and waited down on all fours in the mud trying to pick up any sound over the splattering rain. Just as he thought it was all clear, something touched his butt. A mega-gush of adrenalin dumped into his stomach. It was like a million volts of electricity mixing with fear. He wanted to vomit. He swung around, pistol up, ready to blast. Petunia jumped back, let out a high-pitched whine, and zipped away into the shadows. Jack gagged and swallowed a mouthful of acid, an instant migraine stabbed at the back of his right eye. He sat down in the mud letting the fear burn off, '*fucking mutt.*'

He stood in the shadows of the porch overhang, reaching out with all his senses for anything, sound, smell, movement. The plastic sheeting that had covered the front entrance had been torn open leaving a gap with a wet-black trail leading into the house. The hair on his neck went rigid. He bent and put a finger in the largest pool, it came away sticky with blood. He remained stooped as he went through the door into the dark living room. Halfway in, he tripped over something and went down on his face. He was back up before the pain registered with the pistol out and finger on the trigger searching the room for a target. He felt his way over to the wall, and hit all three switches at the same time. In a flash, the porch, living room, and kitchen lit up like a prison yard, exposing a dead man lying face up with a pool of blood shaped like a halo around his deformed head. A name badge attached to his uniform shirt told Jack it was Deputy Ron Weaver, late of the Monroe County Sheriff's Department. His gun belt was missing along with his shoulder communicator. The bedroom and bath were clear. The bed mattress was gone, presumably taken for Ebola testing. The place smelled of DDT or some type of formaldehyde that the Haz-Mat team must have sprayed to kill the virus. Jack backed out of the room and closed the door. He didn't realize that he had been holding his breath, and he sucked in a lung full of air that left the sticky taste of death in his throat.

Jack eased through Claire's backdoor quietly and tiptoed through the kitchen, alert for trouble. He wanted to take a quick look for anyone hiding in her place. The small house was laid out like his so it was easy to navigate without turning on any lights. The place was neat and organized. His quick inspection didn't find anything amiss. He flipped the deadbolt on his way out.

The alley was dark and wet. A long flash of lightning exploded overhead that made him wince and shield his eyes. The kiloton-jolt turned the alley into day for a moment. No bad guys, no good guys, no squad car. Just him and dead Deputy Weaver.

"Bobbie, it's me," he said into his cell phone as he ducked under his porch to get out of the rain.

"Marsh? Are you at the Hilton?"

"Nah, something came up," he answered. He wiped his head and face with a wad of paper towels. "I'm at my place, it looks like we have trouble. You need to have the Sheriff send some people over here. One of his deputies is down for the count. Looks like a blunt end of a two-by-four hit dead center. That or a howitzer round hit him."

"Marsh Dammit! What is it with you, Ace?" she said, frustrated. "Sit tight, I'll be there in five minutes. Don't touch…"

"Where's Sonny Powers?" Jack butted in.

"We had him moved over to the Navy Base… Hold on, Ace. I know what you're thinking. You are not to leave your place, understood? Don't do it. You stay put, or I swear I'll kick your ass up between your…Marsh? Marsh? *GODAMMIT!*"

Chapter 13

Jack ran over to Duval Street looking for a cab. Nights like this, he knew several would be idling alongside Fast Buck Freddie's Department Store, where they could spot partiers coming out of the bars up and down Duval Street. He looked for Max Simms's taxi but didn't spot it. He wasn't ready to face Max yet after the fight they had while in one of his drunken stupors. He owed Max an apology, but wasn't ready mentally.

He slapped the roof of the first cab in line and jumped in the backseat.

"*Jeezus, Mister!* Scared the crap out of me," the cabbie said, big Adam's apple bouncing up and down as he spoke.

"Let's roll. Take the shortest and fastest way over to the Navy Hospital."

"You local?"

"Yeah."

"Ok, short and fast, Conch rate."

He flashed his old Marine Corp identification card to the rent-a-cop at the small navy base entrance and they were flagged through with a two-fingered salute. The driver pulled around to the temporary prefabs that housed the V.A. clinic. Jack gave him a twenty and slid out of the backseat.

"Hey, Mister, you said you was a local. The ride was a couple of bucks only. I can't take this."

"Keep it. Buy yourself a bowl of gumbo or something. A night like this you need something hot in you."

The parking lot was empty. The rain was bouncing off the blacktop in a deafening staccato. Jack's hunch was that Mad Mike took Deputy Weaver's vehicle and made tracks to the V.A. to rescue his partner, or to shut him up before he spilled his guts. The back lot was empty. He followed the drive around to the front of the Navy's three-story hospital—more of a dispensary and triage stop than the bigger military facilities up on the mainland. One of the three cars parked in front was the rental that Claire had driven over earlier. The rental's doors were locked and the hood cold to the touch. Same for the other cars parked in the lot.

The front lobby was dark and empty, the only light was down by the elevators, throwing shadows around the room. Wet footprints led down the hall, puddled by the elevator doors, then moved on. The Walther felt good in his hand. He walked softly towards the light, passed the elevators down at the end of the hall. A placard pointed to the left, EMERGENCY. To the right, LAB. He had the pistol up and ready as he took the left — the room was empty. A dozen feet back down the corridor he peeked through a set of swinging doors, spotted someone slumped over a desk, blood pooling at his feet. A chill of fear hit Jack as he pulled away from the doors, and stepped to the side with his back clinging to the wall.

Jack sidestepped down to another door and tried the knob. It turned, he pushed it open, and stepped in. He was in a large exam room of some type with another door facing him that was marked TRIAGE. Jack took in a deep breath and jumped into the TRIAGE room, ready to blast anything that moved. Nothing moved. He spotted a makeshift clear plastic tent placed over a person on a gurney with a sign taped to it, QUARANTINE, and peeked inside. The man's throat had been cut, almost severing the head. A steady drip of blood puddled around the gurney's wheels. The smell was awful and Jack gagged as he let the curtain fall back into place. The clipboard that hung from an IV stand marked the dead man as Sonny Powers.

"Claire!"

Jack quickly searched the curtained exam rooms for Claire, expecting to find her body stuffed in one of the rooms. The man slumped over the desk had his throat cut and had bled out over the desktop and floor. Bloody footprints led over to the gurney and then back towards the swinging doors. Jack slammed the doors open and raced back down the hall towards the lab. His heart was pounding like a sledgehammer hitting an anvil, adrenaline pumped oxygen-rich blood to his muscles. His pupils were needle-pricks of sight focused on the lab door. He felt the primal urge to kill.

"Claire," he screamed, as he kicked the lab door open and charged into the room.

Mad Mike had Claire by the hair, pulling her towards a door across the room. Jack snapped off a shot that missed and ricocheted off the tile walls. Burr pulled Claire up close to him and pointed his pistol at Jack. He popped off a round hitting Jack in the arm. Jack had Burr's forehead in his site-blade and took up the trigger slack, a nanosecond away from killing this man. Mad Mike suddenly ducked behind Claire, using her as a shield. In the instant he ducked, Jack ran to him and kicked his kneecap. He fell back dragging Claire with him, popped off a round that hit Jack in the inner thigh staggering him back a few feet.

Claire was hysterical with fear, scratching and clawing at Burr. Suddenly there was a muffled shot, Claire went slack, and slipped to the floor. Jack went blind with rage as Claire's head hit the floor. He jumped forward and hit Burr a glancing blow across the jaw with his pistol. He kicked Burr as hard as he could with his good leg. Jack fell on him and dug talon-like fingers deep into the flesh on his chest, trying to tear at his heart. Burr screamed in pain. His pistol was trapped between their two bodies. He fought like a madman to get away. Jack's fingers dug deeper into Mad Mike's chest. Both were snarling and growling in a primal rage. Burr's teeth sunk into Jack's collarbone. Jack tore deeper into Burr's wet flesh with fingers swollen with adrenaline ….

KABAM!

Jack's side exploded in a sonic wave that rippled out through his body like a tsunami. He fell back unable to make sense of why things suddenly went into slow motion.

KABOOM!

Another supersonic wave of pain shot through him. Burr's grinning bloody face was spinning round and round like a cyclone, going faster and faster, as Jack fell into a black rabbit-hole.

Chapter 14

The world was spinning out of focus as Jack's eyes tried to see who was standing over him. His brain was playing tricks. Flickering images of wraith-like beings hovered close then seemingly drifting away then moving back in. A blurry arm with stubby fingers reached for him as he tried to slap it away, but couldn't find his hands. It took forever for his head to turn to see what it was sticking out of his chest. His brain lazily reported, *'Jack, that's an arrow in your chest. Arapaho, by the looks—*

"We'll give it another day before we move him. Go ahead and pull the tube while he's out, and watch for any bleeding," The Navy doctor instructed.

"Yes sir," the Corpsman responded. "Sir, his friend is in the waiting room. Can he come in?"

"Sure, go ahead, he would be showing symptoms by now if he had the bug. Take down all this tenting as well, he's clean."

"What about the horses?" Jack asked, having no idea why he said that.

Both men laughed. "Cut back on his drip, too. He's having way too much fun, wherever he is," the doctor said as he disappeared from Jack's view.

"Just lay back and relax, Cowboy," the corpsman said as he placed a hand on his chest and yanked the arrow out.

"*Yeooow*!" he screamed. "What the hell was that?"

"*That* was a vacuum tube we put through the chest wall to inflate the lung. One of the bullets clipped your right lung on its way through, collapsing it. You're fine now. The Doc just took a look at it, and you're almost good to go."

"What bullets?"

"You don't remember what happened?"

"Nah...kind of." Memory was flickering on the edges, but he couldn't put it together,

"Is it still raining out?"

"Raining? Oh, you're talking about the tropical front that sat over us for three days."

"Three days! How long have I been here?

"You were in ICU for three days, and you've been up here for two. Time flies when you're sucking morphine like you've been doing," the Corpsman laughed.

"Five days? Oh *fuck*, I've got to get out of here. Where's Burr?"

Jack's pulse redlined as he quickly looked around the room. Everything came back to him in living color. Images of the lab and the struggle with Burr. Claire screaming in terror, then collapsing. The burning pain from the gunshots in his chest and hip. He collapsed back, trying to get himself under control.

"Claire! Oh God, Claire, I'm so sorry," he cried softly.

His whole being filled with agony at the thought that it was his fault she was dead. "What have I done.... what have I done?" He couldn't hold back the sobs that shook his body in anguish.

"Take it easy, Mr. Marsh. Doctor Marlow is alive, she survived the gunshot. There are major complications though. She was transferred up to Miami a few days ago; she needed surgery on her spinal cord. Most of her female plumbing came out because of the damage the bullet caused. The bad news is that she's in a coma. The bullet entered her back, shattering two vertebrae, and nicked the spinal cord."

"She's alive?" Jack asked, relief flooding through him. "Thank God! Coma? As in asleep?"

"Yeah, like sleep, except she can't wake up. The specialists all say that she has a fifty-fifty chance of coming around. Right now, she is on life support to help her breathe. Everyone is just waiting now to see if she can pull herself back."

"Oh, at least she has a chance. I've got to get up there to see her."

"Take it easy sir, you're not going anywhere yet. Her family was notified, and her husband is with her now. He arrived…"

"Husband! Husband!" Jack croaked loudly. He didn't hear correctly. There is no husband. Why did he say that?

"You're mistaken, she doesn't have a husband, she's not married," he blurted out. "It's Burr, he's after her, she's in danger."

"Hold on, sir, lay back down, you're going to open those incisions. Lay back now."

"But…. She's…"

"Well, I don't know any Burr, but the guy with her is Doctor Roger Marlow, head of cardiology at Catholic Hospital in Milwaukee. He's been by her side through all the procedures; I don't know what else to tell you."

Jack lay staring at the ceiling, his eyes vacant, ears roaring with the sound of blood pumping through his broken heart, his wounds forgotten. He was suspended in time, sanity dangling from a thread tied to something he couldn't see. Jack's hands shook with wino-tremors; his stomach was a witch's cauldron of boiling acid. His body shuddered, he gagged as bile spewed out over his chest and dressings. He continued to gag for several minutes and then collapsed back, weak from the episode. Several corpsmen circled him dabbing and wiping, checking his wounds for any contamination. He felt a pinprick in his arm and peacefully slipped away from the hustle and bustle around him.

It was nighttime, his room was bright with star-shine, the hum of the central air was calming. His sheets were tucked under his chin, arms nestled up under his head. The hospital smells were strangely comforting. He was thinking of his Mother and how much he missed her. She was always the strong one in the family; nothing ever seemed to throw her off track. If she ever hurt, she kept it to herself and never let on that she was troubled. The only time Jack ever knew her to waiver was when the notice came that he had been wounded in Kuwait. His aunt told him later that his mother read the notice several times, slumped against the front door, then calmly pulled herself together saying, "I'm going to skin that boy good when I get my hands on him. If I know him, he probably winged a couple before they got him."

Other memories flickered in and out, like an old 16 mm movie camera, jerky and out of focus. Jack managed to slow the speed down to a crawl and smiled big when he thought of Tyrone standing in Mama Dey's living room telling her that he wasn't getting on any airplane that night or any other night, and Mama reaching up on her tippy-toes, twisting his ear until he cried out, *I'll go, I'll go.*

'You ain't just a toot'n you're going, even if I have to conjure up something or other. I just don't know what God was thinking when he gave you such a powerful Shine. Seems like a waste to me. Now go get yourself together....and put on them trousers that got the buttons in front, that zipper on the other pair is broke. Suffer the chilrun, Lord.'

So now, here he was, flat on his back with a couple of bullet holes in his hide, Burr's trail was cold, and a broken heart. Seems like he spent most of his life in this same predicament. The good news was though, every time, he managed to live through it. He always came out the other side a little more battered, a little more callous, and a little more scarred. This time, he decided, he was finished with trying to be a hero to everyone and every cause that came along.

Jack cleared his mind and drifted off on a morphine cloud.

"Is it alive?" Tom asked, as he poked Jack in the ribs.

"Ouch! Stop! That hurts," Jack said, snapping awake.

His eyes felt puffy and sticky. He squinted from the bright sunshine pouring into the room. Tom was standing at the side of the bed, big grin on his mug, with a paper cup of coffee.

"Throw this down, you'll feel much better. Then get your butt up, we've got things to do and places to go, Private Marsh."

"I'm not going anywhere except to the head, then I'm checking out of this house of pain and going home. I've declared victory, the war is over, I'm heading back to CONUS on the first freedom flight out."

"Not so fast my friend, the war *ain't* over, and you *ain't* going back nowhere, until we finish up down south. You got us into this mess and now *you're* going to stick around and help clean it up...."

"Me? I got us into this mess? Are you nuts or something? *You* came to *me*, begging *me* to help an old Marine buddy out, *'Please Jacky, I owe him Jacky, he saved my life, Jacky.'* I'm the one that said the whole thing stunk, and let's *not* get involved."

"Whatever," Tom said dismissively. "That's history. We're up to our necks in it now and you ain't pulling out on me. Big trouble's brewing down south, and we need all the guns we can get on the firing line."

"What's happening that's so bad you need my immediate help? I have a couple of new holes in me, in case you haven't noticed. I need some downtime to heal" Jack felt burned out, he honestly didn't think he could take much more. "Tom, look at me, I'm burned up, I don't have another round in me, I'm down for the count...."

Tom stared into Jack's eyes for a few moments. "Yeah, maybe you're right, Jack. Go on home and get better. You don't need to be involved in this. I never should have pulled you in anyway. I don't want you to get hurt any more than you already have," Tom said. His face wrinkled with worry.

He squeezed Jack's hand tight and wiped at the corner of his eye. "The guys will understand..."

"*Damnit, Tom! Stop*! I'll go, I'll go, just stop with the phony BS, but I swear after this I'm gone. Do you hear me?"

"Jackie, I knew I could count on you. You've never run from a fight in your life. Since when has a couple of bullet holes ever slowed a Marine down? We're tough, Jackie, bad to the bone, mean machines, son…"

"Ok, Ok, Tom, I'm in," He said fending off the tough-guy barrage, "Now tell me what I'm walking into. What's happened the last few days that's so urgent that you need the walking wounded to help out?

"It ain't pretty Jack."

Chapter 15

The ultra-modern glass and aluminum structure that housed Wade Preston's exploration conglomerate was a gemstone compared to the other businesses along the Houston ship channel. Most of the surrounding area was old, rundown warehouses, rusting equipment, cranes, nets, and piping. Piping that ran for miles in an insane Etch-A-Sketch pattern leading from dockside to chemical refineries, back to the docks…back to refineries. Oil, gasoline, and by-products flowed through these miles of pipes then somehow, at the end of the month, the in-flow and out-flow was tallied up, and each business operating on the channel smiled all the way to the bank. There were no unprofitable companies in the oil business, some were just run smarter than others, and then, some were mismanaged more than others.

Wade Preston learned years before that to make it big in the oil business, one had to diversify and not depend on just one or two petroleum products to survive. To cover himself, he branched out into the oilrig platform construction and leasing business. He also put together a deep-water salvage and recovery business as a way to even out cash flow during lean times like embargoes and war. Those Middle East camel jockeys didn't play fair most of the time. Most people think gasoline, when they think of *Big Oil*. That's true, all the major gasoline companies are the storefronts for the industry, while thousands of smaller unknown companies make fortunes off the chemical by-products produced that touch every single living person in the world on a daily basis. The idea of industrialized countries eliminating oil for a more nebulous green power source to save the planet is so naïve, and so irresponsible that it borders on criminal. Preston knew that the political power players had not thought out, nor understood, the risks to world stability an unplanned shift would cause.

Preston saw the U.S. President as the drum major marching the country to energy collapse and an unrecoverable economic disaster through his push for unproven and unsustainable trade-offs. His executive orders pushing wind energy, soy, switch-grass, sugar cane, corn, and voluntary public cutbacks and usage were crazy. Sure, you could use all of these, but not as sustainable energy sources. Experts in the energy industry knew that the worlds basic power sources, oil, coal, natural gas, solar, nuclear, would be needed until a viable replacement had been proven as effective and sustaining. That replacement, in the minds of the experts, would be the hydrogen fuel cell. Until then, the current energy will need to come from where it has always come from, deep in the earth.

Preston exhaled a mouth full of rancid cigar smoke, and spit out a bit of tobacco leaf that landed on the polished desk in front of Mad Mike Burr, both men stared at the tidbit for a moment. A macho insult or an unspoken power play? The moment slid by unchallenged.

"You and your friend really fucked up down in Key West. You're down there for less than three days, and manage to terrorize the place, killing everyone but the target."

"Don't tell me my business, Mr. Preston. You wanted me to move fast. Things get fucked up when you're on a clock. Let me do it my way and this would be over. That wet-brain Marsh was lucky. Don't worry about him; his ass and his hoodoo friends are all going down."

"Yeah, like Austin Burke was going down. The easiest target you will ever have. He escaped in the night, buck-assed naked through one of Houston's affluent neighborhoods and you guys lose him. Maybe I have the wrong man working for me, Mike. Maybe, I need to go back up to Huntsville, and get me a new boy. Somebody with a steady hand and who doesn't have a problem following through."

Burr's face went pale. His pulse beat visibly at his temple. The hired killer's eyes went a mysterious yellow with red-flecks. He locked on his target, a nanosecond away from striking out. Preston inwardly shuddered as he realized he might have gone too far and immediately reversed course.

"On the other hand, I feel confident I have the right man right here to do the job. I've just been pushing too hard to get this mess under control. You're right; you need a little leeway to pull off a major hit like this. You know me, always trying to micro manage things, Heh, Heh," Preston said, leaning forward and flicking the tidbit of tobacco away from Burr and off the desktop.

"Let's rethink this and see what our options are. If I had to reprioritize our game plan, I would say that Austin Burke is still target-one since he discovered the gold and is undoubtedly working on a plan to get it up. That idiot Chandler was a loose cannon. Burke never should have let him come to Houston; he should have kept him under his thumb. The idiot's not here an hour and he's told everyone about the billions in gold. There are no secrets in this business, Mike. That was a good job you did on him. I won't forget it. As for the others: the crew, Tom Parker, and Jack Marsh are speedbumps that are in our way, but as far as a threat, nah. They need to go because they can come up behind us later and point fingers."

"Mr. Preston, I've lost a few days because I underestimated my enemy. That won't happen again. I never fuck up twice. The trail is cold, but I can pick it back up. In fact, I already have a couple of friends sniffing around. I'm not going to tell you what my plan is in advance, but you'll know when things happen."

"That's sounds just fine to me. The less I know the better off I am. I don't need to be at your operational level. To show my confidence in you, I am doubling your payday. Whatever your new helpers are costing, I'll cover that too. Just understand that when this thing is over, I don't want anyone, or anything standing that can ever come back to me. And Mike, you and I will never meet again. Clear?"

"That's the way I see it too. I'm giving you a heads up now so you can protect yourself. My plan is for most of what is about to go down will happen in Jamaica. That includes Marsh, Parker, and anyone else who gets in the way," Mad Mike said with a wicked smile. "And Wade, just so we both understand each other, wire the rest of my money today. I won't be coming back this way unless you try to cross me."

Chapter 16

The small frame house in Pasadena looked just like the other two hundred surrounding it in a ten-block hovel called Bay View Estates. Considering there wasn't a bay within thirty miles of the blue-collar neighborhood, the developer removed the billboard sign immediately upon completion of the tract. Now the locals just referred to the place as Bay View. The surrounding refineries spewed toxic waste down on Bay View and the rest of Pasadena twenty-four hours a day. Kids living in Bay View generally didn't contribute much to the states scholastic scores anyway, so no one really gave a shit if they were healthy or not.

The death smell from the small frame house mixing in with the surrounding polluted air went unnoticed. Mad Mike recognized the scent immediately as he entered the living room. He drew in a deep breath, let it out slowly, enjoying the acrid tang of death. An electrode sparked somewhere deep inside, tingled for a moment, then passed.

"Rabbit, are we finished here?" Burr yelled, as he looked around the neatly kept living room and kitchen. He knew that the home belonged to Jim Taylor. the *Sea Bird's* third mate, who now lay dead in the back bedroom.

When Mad Mike Burr recruited Sonny Powers to help kill Jack Marsh in Key West a few days ago, Jim Taylor had turned him down. Not because of the dirty work, but because Jim wanted to stay home to drink and screw until it was time to report back to the *Sea Bird.* After leaving Wade Preston's office, Mad Mike had a hunch that Jim may have heard from Austin Burke and knew his whereabouts. A quick trip over to *Stinkadena* as the locals called it, seemed like the best place to start to pick up Burke's trail. He wouldn't escape this time.

Taylor's wife, Linda, had watched her man being slowly tortured to death by Mad Mike's new crew, Rabbit Reynolds, and E.Z. Smith, both ex-cons from Huntsville's high-risk lockdown. Both men bounced out of prison early for time-served and at the convenience of the State of Texas. Once released, they disappeared into the wind, going back to the only thing they knew, violent crime.

"Where's E.Z.?" Mad Mike asked.

"In back, doing the woman again. Bitch's been unconscious for the last five hours, but that don't stop the Z-Man. He says he's trying to improve on his technique."

Burke walked over to the front bedroom, watched E.Z. for a minute, then popped him on the butt with a towel,

"Finish up, Z, we got work to do."

Fifteen minutes later, Rabbit was shaking powdered lye out of a fifty-pound bag over Jim and Linda Taylor's bodies stacked in the bathtub.

"Lye powder is good for fig trees." Z said. "I learned that when I was working the garden squad outside the main walls That's the time I killed that little sissy-boy. He says to me, 'Know the name of these figs?' I say no, and he says, 'Black Sweet Turkeys…. gobble-gobble'. I just lost it man, took three Bulls to pull me off that sumbitch."

"Yeah, it's good for eating up dead people, too. Now bust open that other bag so we can get out of here. This crap's nasty if it gets in your nose and eyes."

The three ex-cons piled into the cab of Jim Taylor's pickup just as it was getting dark and rolled over to Interstate 610. Before leaving the Taylor house, Mad Mike parked Cara Morrison's Toyota coupe in the Taylor's garage, and locked the big sliding door tight with a hasp combo-lock he had picked up at K-Mart. Cara's nude body was tucked under a blanket in the trunk, her head resting peacefully on the spare tire.

'Within two hours of Linda Taylor telling EZ and Rabbit how she had told Cara Morrison, Burke's secretary, about Burr's plans to hit somebody in Key West, Burr and Rabbit had broken into Austin Burke's office, found out where Cara lived, and had her tied up nude on the bedroom floor of her condominium. Cara confessed that Austin Burke had been staying with her for the last few days after he escaped the motel. She told the two cons how Austin spent the time following the shootings related to Jack Marsh in Key West. Austin had flown out that morning to Jamaica to hook up with Tiny Miles on the Sea Bird Explorer as a safe haven to work from as things continued to unfold. Once Burr felt satisfied that Cara had told him everything, he signaled Rabbit to join him in the living room,

'I think we have everything she knows. I'll take it from here. Take the rental car back to Taylor's place. I'll follow later in the girl's car. Meanwhile, squeeze Taylor and his old lady for anything on Burke or the gold. We'll use their place as a safe house until we can get a flight to Kingston.'

'You sure you don't need any help with the girl?' Rabbit asked, craning his neck around the bedroom door, trying to sneak a peek. Burr didn't answer, just gave Rabbit a little shove to the front door.

Later on, as Burr sat in Wade Preston's office discussing his plans for finishing off the assignment that Wade had given him, he had a deep visceral thrill knowing that Cara's dead body was just outside Wade's place of business, as Wade played his macho power games. Power? This idiot didn't have a clue to what real power was.

Chapter 17

The taxi ride from Miami International to Aventura Hospital took a little over an hour because of mid-day traffic on I-95. Jack's mind was like a Rubik's cube on speed-dial, twisting, turning, thinking three, four moves ahead, spinning, and rotating. Why was he here? What was he going to accomplish? It was over. She's married, for Christ sake! Why do this to himself? The same answer came back every time. Jack, you love her. She's in critical condition because of you. If she died with you not checking on her, you would never be able to face yourself again.

The cabbie pulled up to the hospital's main entrance with his horn blaring at an old lady using a walker, motioning for her to hurry up and move it.

"That just cost you your tip," Jack said as he counted out the exact amount of the fare, and handed it to the driver, slamming the door hard. He looked over his shoulder as the cab sped away, honking, flipping him off, and calling out dirty names in some Island language, '*Ah Miami, the Creole melting pot.*'

The nurse's desk on the fourth floor was a bird's nest of plump nightingales, flitting about with clipboards, IV trolleys, linens, syringes, and the odd coffee mug. Jack made his way to the counter, not sure how to proceed,

"Jack Marsh here to see Doctor Marlowe please."

"I haven't seen him for a while," the nurse answered looking about. "He might be in the cafeteria."

"Oh, I'm sorry. I meant Doctor Claire Marlow. Not her husband," he said.

"Are you a member of the family, Mr. Marsh?"

"Well, actually I'm just a close friend who desperately needs to see Claire. I'm going away for a while and I just want to peek in on her, just for a second. Please."

Like most nurses, this one had a sixth sense that there was more to this man's request than just that of a friend bearing flowers. She looked up and down the halls,

"I can't say for sure, but if one were to stand in front of 429 for a few minutes, an opportunity might open up for someone to take a quick peek inside, if one were so inclined, and if one denied that there were any co-conspirators involved."

With this said she spun around and submerged her head in a giant rolodex filled with charts.

Jack was down the hall and in front of 429 in two seconds flat, then inside the room in less than that. The room was cold and dimly lit. The only light coming from the various life support machines and equipment attached to Claire.

"Oh Claire, I'm so sorry," he said as he stood over her stroking her hand. She appeared to be in a deep restful sleep with just a hint of color on her cheeks. Her eyelids fluttered a little as her mind played out some unknown drama that only she could see.

"I just stopped by to see you for a minute, and to tell you everything is ok between you and me. We all have secrets and sometimes they hurt more than help. God knows, I have more secrets than a man should. My secrets are all the kind that hurt people. I am so ashamed of me, Claire, and the things I have done to others in the past. I just wanted to say that I know you must have had your reasons for not giving me a heads-up on the husband and all, and that's ok. You just get better. Just watch, you'll be up and out of here in no time."

Jack couldn't go on. He hurt so much inside he thought he was going to break. He took Mama Dey's little hairball with the grain of sand inside and placed it in her hand and folded it closed. She needed all the help she could get, and if that little fleck of sand from some ancient place could help her, then it was hers. He stepped back from the bed, wiping his eyes.

"Hey, if you're ever in Key West again look me up, I'll buy you a drink." He turned and walked out.

"Mr. Marsh? Jack Marsh?" A big handsome guy in a doctor's clinical jacket asked.

"Yeah, I'm Marsh," Jack said feeling caught trespassing.

"I'm Roger Marlow, Claire's husband. Can we talk for a moment?"

"Sure, Doc, what's on your mind?" For some reason, Jack liked this guy. He would have liked to punch him in the nose for claiming his wife back, but he let it pass.

"I understand you've been through quite a bit yourself, a couple of bullet holes, a bad concussion, unconscious for a day or so. That must have been one hell of a fight you and Claire got caught up in."

"It's not over yet, Doc, I just stopped by to peek in on Claire before I head out to track the mutt down and finish the job. Payback is going to be tough on him."

"I was told you are one tough son-of a bitch, Jack. I'd hate to have you on my trail. Before you go, there is something you should know regarding Claire and me. Claire left me almost two years ago because of my…flings, as she called them. I guess I *flung* one too many times and she packed up and headed for happier grounds. Long story short, we're in the process of getting divorced. We tried to make it work several times, but I guess I'm just an old street dog and can't keep it at home. I know I'll never change. Even though I love Claire very much, I'll always be out sniffing around."

Jack was holding his breath. He felt lightheaded. He gulped and stammered,

"Divorced? You mean it's over between you two? I can take her on the cruise she and I talked about? She can go back to Key West?" The words just flowed out in a rush of relief, '*a reprieve, no Jesus needle, I'm going to live, she's mine.*'

"So, Roger, exactly when does the divorce become final?" he asked nonchalantly.

"Don't worry Jack, It's going through. We just need to get her better now, then everything else will follow."

"Well yes, of course, we need to concentrate on her, and then the three of us can finalize everything."

"After meeting you, Jack, believe me, I think she has found the kind of man she deserves and needs. You have my blessing," he said as he stood up and patted him on the back. "You go get that son-of-a bitch who did this to her and I'll take care of her from this end. Deal?" he said, sticking his hand out.

"Deal," Jack said.

He went back inside Claire's room and kissed her softly on the cheek. He was about to explode with happiness. His tears of joy wet her cheeks as they fell from his eyes. He wiped her face with a tissue, kissed her one last time, and backed out of the room. Roger was nowhere in sight as he hurried down the hall, anxious to do his part of the bargain.

Chapter 18

Several vendors had set up makeshift sidewalk shops across the street from Ritha Troupe's house in Spanish Town, a ghetto suburb of Kingston, using pieces of tarp canvas, umbrellas, or just open-air tables. The vendors sold ice-cold drinks, sugar cane sticks, sliced watermelon, and fresh papayas to the gawkers who had camped out around Ritha's place. Hawkers were selling juju of every description, kids sat curbside quietly with their mothers waiting for something to happen, and a parade of people passed slowly watching for some magical sign of what was going on inside. Others hurried by, not wanting any part of the rumors that had spread across the Island.

Inside Sister Ritha's house were three of the most powerful Caribbean spiritualist forces in all of the Islands, as well as Africa itself, some said. Mama Dey was from the oldest village in Africa that went back even before the River Village. She had powers to call up good or evil spirits from the *Nsari,* the river that swallows all rivers, the home of all *Loas*, Divine Spirits. Oola Dey had psychic powers that gave her visions of things past and things coming. Oola had special powers of *Mbula*, which protects and fights against evil spirits and their imps. The people of Jamaica who practiced *Obeah* and *Kumina,* versions of Vodum or voodoo in particular, viewed Oola as a High Priestess among the spiritual *Loas*, divine spirits. She was their living Black Saint that worked tirelessly to protect her people from evil spirits

Tyrone Crawford, the simple man with the gift of the *Shine* from New Iberia, Louisiana, lay on the same bed where Lamont Troupe had lain in death only a week ago.

Tyrone however was very much alive, albeit in a deep coma induced by hypnosis and one of Mama Dey's concoctions. His body was in constant motion, twitching, mumbling, and uttering an occasional cry of pain. In his current state, he was Ty Obi, a descendent of the *Loa, Saka,* and Spiritual warrior of good against evil. The disease and pestilence facing the Islands was in Ty Obi's hands against an even stronger force rooted in the Body of Dorothea Lapin, Jacques Lapin's mother. The Baboon himself was present in her body and was prepared to fight to the death to get loose among the living again.

Mr. Rene Renaud, a small dwarf of a man from Haiti, had arrived the night before from Port Au Prince, bringing the disturbing news that the Devil Blood was spreading among the Haitian locals in remote pockets of that country.

"The local authorities have traced the sickness along Highway 3 through the mountain pass leading into the Dominican Republic, down the Sanchez Main Highway and into Santo Domingo, the capital of the D.R. If there is any sickness inside of the D.R., they are keeping it very quiet." Mr. Renaud wiped his baldhead and sweaty face with a huge red bandana.

Oola Dey was alarmed at the news of the spread of the Ebola, and knew it could easily jump from island to island,

"Monsieur Renaud, what is the real purpose of visiting us? Why not go to the health authorities? This is indeed troubling news and must be given to the authorities immediately. If not contained, the fever could kill thousands."

"Madam, I am not here on behalf of the authorities. They are being notified through the proper channels. I was sent to tell you that the source of the disease is already inside of Jamaica and is hidden somewhere nearby. I am but a messenger. Our own Mama Madeleine, High Priestess of all Voodoo in Haiti and Port Au Prince, sends this message to you, Madam, and to Mama Dey." The little man's face went slack, his eyes rolled back in his head where only the whites showed, and he began to speak in a clear feminine voice,

"Sisters, Mbula, protector against ill will, Moganga the Benevolent, Nganga Diviners of the words of the Ancient Ones, peace to you. The Old Baboon is among us again. He is strong, and has many followers. It was prophesied in the Old Village that the Baboon would escape someday, and destroy the Original People of the land. This is not his time, although he thinks it is. He must be chained again, and cast into the River that eats all Rivers. This is your task. He is feasting inside a fat Kakwa woman who teaches Mpendla, the drinking of human blood, and the eating of flesh to her followers. Her son DaDa is the instrument of the Baboons escape. Both of these evil spirits must be purged and tormented until their bodily hosts are Zombies, and left empty. It will be difficult, and will take all of your powers, but we must prevail. My Sisters, I am sending four warriors to surround you during this struggle. They will appear this day, unseen to most, seen by the evil ones as a warning to

stay away. This is a struggle among the very Gods of the People. Bless you, my most sacred Sisters in Santeria."

The dwarf fell over deep in a trance. The room was silent as the man lay breathing deeply and speaking in an ancient African tongue,

"Shhh!" Sister Ritha said. "He saying something."

All three women got on their knees to hear what the messenger was saying,

"Dead bodies from the trees come by the sea /

Secret so dark, no one can see/

cold holds them in sleep/

soon it come clear and they be free /

then death will come for you and me"

"Gracious me," Mama Dey said, as she spit on the dwarf.

Oola Dey was subconsciously rolling her scrawny shoulders with little chicken wing flaps of her elbows, clucking softly, Sister Ritha sat back on her haunches petrified at not knowing what had been said, but could feel that the temperature in the room had dropped at least ten degrees.

Mama Dey suddenly grabbed a broom and started beating the little gnome on the floor. As he came out of his trance, he rolled around the small room trying to escape the heavy blows, covering his head with his small arms, ducking and dodging.

"You bringing evil messages to this holy house. You shut your mouth. Get out now, go where that evil talk come from."

"Don't hit me, I'm just the messenger. Whoever's out there and wants to say something they just plop it in my mouth. I can't stop it."

"*Out! Now!* You the devil's imp," she yelled, as she physically picked up the little man and threw him out the screen door into the yard. "Git! You be gone from this here Island, or I send a pack a dogs straight from hell after you," Mama yelled, as the man scampered out of the yard, scattering the crowd in a panic.

Mama took a couple of swipes at the dusty porch to rid it of anything the dwarf left behind, clucking under her breath. As she turned to go back inside, her eye caught an unusual sight over in one corner of the yard. A very tall thin young man, at least six and a half feet, maybe seven foot, stood looking out at the crowd, as if on sentry duty, a rough-woven red cloth thrown over one shoulder, the other shoulder was bare, a long thin staff in his hand. She quickly glanced over to the other corner of the yard, same thing, a tall man on sentry duty. She rubbed her eyes with boney knuckles and looked back a moment later, and they were gone.

"I'm getting old, my old eyes playing games on me. Ain't no Maasai Warriors around here. Just crazy words from

Madam Madelaine, she's always conjuring up stuff that ain't there," she said, as she shook her head and went back inside.

Chapter 19

As the moon rose over the mountains to the east, and evening lights were coming on in small villages and towns around the Island, the sound of drums could be heard from afar and near. All sending the same message of alert. It didn't matter what your beliefs were: Christian, Rasta, Voodoo, Obeah, or Kumina, when the drums spoke, the people listened. Tonight's message warned people to stay at home, spirits were out and about tonight that usually only appeared for religious or festive occasions, like Carnival, celebrating the changing seasons, or good omens. It was being drummed that ancient forces were in play, and unless you had business out and about, you stay home shuttered up with your family.

Dorothea Lapin's small house in the mountains was lit by a wax candle placed on a small keg that served as a table. The house was empty. Two hundred yards behind her house, in a natural grotto in the jungle, a bonfire was raging with men and women dancing around the fire to the beat of primal drums. The dancers, all dressed in white shifts, swayed with exaggerated movements, some falling to the ground shaking, eyes rolled back in their heads. A dozen women chanted a repetitive plaintiff to the spirits in keening voices, words from some long-ago African village. Several goats tied to stakes bleated in fear, knowing that no good was coming their way. A woman stood with a rooster held out in one hand and cut its throat with the other. The rooster's blood splashed the dancers, which drove them to even more frenzied shaking and trembling.

A bare-chested man stepped forward, a rod in his hand, a skull on the end, feathers fluttering. A large phallic-shaped gourd was fitted around his waist. The grotto fell silent. The dancers collapsed where they were. The woman with the chicken laid its carcass across a small altar, lit up by bowls of bees wax and then faded into the shadows. The man walked among the prone bodies surrounding the fire.

"This one." He tapped a young woman on the chest with his skull staff. Two men emerged from the shadows and carried the woman inside a grass hut set back from the circle.

"This one," the man tapped another young woman and she was carried into the shack.

A third woman was chosen and taken inside.

For the next ten minutes, the only sound was of the fire crackling, and the bleating of the doomed goats. The cloth-drape covering the hut's door was pushed aside and Dorothea *Jomo,* High Priestess of *Mpendla,* the Spirit of Death, emerged carrying a large calabash bowl held out in front of her. She sat the bowl on the altar placed between her and the bonfire. A Shaman threw a handful of powder on the fire and a flash of bright light lit up the sweaty faces. All eyes were on Dorothea *Jomo.*

"The three chosen ones were indeed in their cycle. I have gathered their issue as an offering tonight to *Mpendla,*

The Spirit of Darkness, and the salvation of our Black People on earth. Tonight, he is among us. His time is near, my children. I can feel his heart beat next to mine. Come, share in his feast of life giving blood." As she said this, she raised the gourd and drank. Soon, there was a line of men and women waiting their turn for a taste of the maidens' offering. As they drank, the drums started their beat again, and the dancers swooned and swayed. Shortly, couples were running off into the surrounding jungle to mate among the tree spirits. The goats were butchered and roasted; the feasting went on into the early hours of morning.

The dark path back to Dorothea's small house was familiar to her, and even though it was a moonless night, she knew every step of the way. The revelers had mostly gone home after the dancing and feasting died down, while some of the younger couples were still out in the bushes. Dorothea chuckled at the thought, and remembered her own days as a young priestess who could have her pick of any of the young males in her *Church*.

She was almost to the clearing behind her house, by the chicken coops, when she sensed a force around her. She clutched at the juju around her neck. The small sack contained a cat's eye and a baby's ear, and she trusted it to tell her what they saw and heard. Dorothea tilted her head to hear better. A blanket was thrown over her body. She felt a sting on her arm that made her cry out as rough hands trussed her up. She was carried struggling around to the front of her house and tossed in the bed of a truck. Then blackness enveloped her. Four big men sat on Dorothea as she unconsciously thrashed around, one second moaning, the next snarling, and the next howling. Finally, the huge woman, and whatever it was driving her to such a frenzy, succumbed to the narcotic.

The rest of the ride to the small village of Ocho Rio was uneventful. The truck pulled off the main highway, drove down a washed out dirt road for a quarter of a mile, and pulled up to a small house set back in a small clearing. The house was actually more of a hut, with clapboard walls, and a tin roof with a porch running around it. This was Oola Dey's house and temple. Not many visitors ventured back to the hut very often unless they had a specific need or help. Seclusion is what Oola and Mama Dey wanted for what they had to do. The next twenty-four hours would be crucial to stopping the spread of the blood fever and to send the Baboon back to the river.

The truck pulled around behind the small hut and stopped in front of an airline cargo-igloo—airlines around the world use these to place luggage and loose cargo in below the passenger space to keep the luggage from shifting. This igloo had been stolen earlier in the evening from the Montego Bay Airport and the chances were it would never be missed…. or found.

The four men struggled to pull Dorothea off the truck bed, then unceremoniously rolled her inside the aluminum container. Once she was inside, Mama Dey threw in bundles of salt grass, ganja weed soaked in urine, a dead dog, a crucifix with the Black Christ affixed upside down, and several pots of burning herbs. The doors were closed and the handles placed in the locked position. The four men piled in the pickup truck and drove off back towards Montego Bay, spitting over their shoulders to ward off any spirits that may have hopped along for the ride.

Tyrone Crawford sat in a rocking chair on the back porch of the hut, staring off into the night. Several crates of chickens sat alert, anxiously waiting to see what the future held for them. A pie-eyed dog with three legs nosed around for table scraps without any luck. Tyrone knew that this dog was special to all *Loa*. This particular dog was holy. He was believed to be the descendant of one of their own village people who had traded his Kingdom to become a dog so his family would be spared from the wars with the Original People during ancient times.

"Our People's history is mostly gone, Mr. Dog King, but what a story, if it was ever told," Tyrone said, as he scratched the dog's ears. "Yes indeedy, what a story, mmm hmm."

Chapter 20

A freshening wind out of the east was forecast to bring showers overnight across the Island, with a slow moving tropical low to follow over the next couple of days. Rain, she was a coming. The airports in Kingston and Montego were operating at full capacity with commercial and private aircraft of every description arriving hourly with tourists. Hotels and resorts were booked to capacity. High Season for the cruise lines had the port terminals packed, with more ships swinging on their anchor chains in the harbors. Local merchants were busy marking up prices on tourist goods, bars and restaurants were doubling their staffs. The Posses were busy cutting dime bags, Pimp-Daddy's were licking their chops, and their girls were ready to put in long hours. Good times were coming to the Island.

Jack was standing back in the alley's shadows across the street from the hostel where Mad Mike Burr and his two gun-monkeys were staying. Bobbie stepped out of the hostel's front door and motioned him over.

"The clerk says that three men matching the description of Burr and his two men are in room two-twenty. As far as he knows they are in the room now," she said softly.

"Let's take 'em."

"Jack, remember I'm not here and was never with you if Captain Price ever asks."

"Bobby, we've been over this a dozen times. If you are going to follow orders to watch over me then you have to go and do what I do. Now, if you feel uncomfortable about taking on some bad people, then I'll understand and you can wait for me here in the alley."

"You calling me a sissy, Ace?" Bobbie popped her knuckles menacingly. "What I said was to never tell Price I was here with you. I didn't say I wasn't going up there with you."

"Let's roll then."

They walked into the tiny lobby, which was nothing more than a registration desk and two old guest chairs with a coffee table between them. The clerk held up his hands.

"I don't want to get nobody hurt, so if y'all here to cause trouble then I'm calling the constable."

"No trouble, Bro, we're here to visit a couple of friends, that's all," Jack said, and slipped him a couple of fifties. "If you hear any noise it will be us just all happy to see each other," he said, and threw him a piece sign.

"Whitey Mon words no good, just don't shoot me on your way out," the guy implored, shaking his head, making the huge watermelon knit-hat he was wearing sway back and forth, as if it had a life of its own.

Halfway up the stairs, they stopped and checked their weapons then started back up. On the second floor landing the hallway was narrow with room doors every dozen feet or so, indicating the rooms were small. T.V.s were playing, people talking, bedsprings screaming, the usual fleabag hotel sounds. Jack's senses were so wired he could almost pick up Radio Free Havana, even his hair follicles were sending danger feelers out. Bobby was in front hugging the wall with her pistol up and ready. Jack was right behind her, half turned, watching their back. The plan was to go in blasting anything that moved then get back out before the sound finished echoing off the walls.

They were across from room two-sixteen when a door opened and a small weasel-faced guy stepped out of two-twenty, took one look at them, slammed the door, opened the door back up and popped off two rounds. Bobbie went down hard, not moving. Jack rushed the door and kicked with all his might, shooting as he went in.

He went in low and rolled right. Weasel-face was sitting against the far wall with a bullet hole next to his nose, below the eye. A big black guy wearing a wife-beater t-shirt was standing by the window pointing a pistol at Jack's head. A flame shot out from the muzzle. Jack zigged to the left. The round tore a fist-sized hole in the wall behind him. Another figure appeared from the bathroom door, pushed the black dude out of the way, and jumped out the window. Burr, that chicken shit. Jack popped three rounds into the big guy just as he went for the window.

Bobbie appeared in the doorway with her pistol up and ready, her shirt was scorched and burning where the bullet hit her vest. Jack was surprised, but glad to see her.

"Get down on the street. I'm going after Burr," he screamed.

He ran to the window, pushed the big guy out, and heard the body hit trashcans in the alley below. Jack was out right behind him, landed on his side, and screamed in pain as a scabbed-over exit wound tore open, *"Fuck!"*

Jack watched a shadowy figure running down the alley and raised his pistol to crank off a round, but the pain in his side was like a sledgehammer. He dropped his arm and ran after the shadow.

The alley let out on Queen Street. Dozens of people out shopping, running errands, and strolling, crowded the road. Tourists were everywhere, laughing, drinking, getting a head start on the night's festivities. Burr stopped running to better mix in with the foot traffic. Jack could see him as he limped along behind him, fifty feet back.

Burr was jittery and kept looking over his shoulder to see if someone was following him. He turned left into Market Alley and disappeared among the throngs of shoppers and stalls of every kind and description. Jack stopped and stood on a wood crate to see better, but knew he didn't have much of a chance spotting him in the crowd. Burr could even be doubling back, and he may not spot him until it was too late.

Jack's wound was soaking his shirt and pants with fresh blood. People were starting to point and stare, making a wide birth around him. He decided to cut his losses and get away to tend his wound.

Back on Queen's Street, he flagged a pedi-cab and hopped on the back. Typically, locals rode on the bandit-taxi mopeds because of the cheap fare. With a Whitey-Mon on the back, the young Rasta driver was determined to make it a ride his passenger would never forget. Jack hung onto the driver's waist with one hand and his side with the other. After three blocks of death-defying stunts, Jack pulled out his pistol and stuck it under the man's chin.

"Slow this fucker down or that watermelon hat you got on is going to be full of Rasta shit," he shouted into the wind shear.

"Wha? Say What? You ain't got to pull no gun, Whitey Mon, Jacob just having some fun. Put that boom-boom away, I'll take you where you want to go."

And that's how Jack met Jacob Kwame, bandit cab driver, tour guide, Island historian, entrepreneur, and totally insane.

Jacob looked him up and down as he raised the pair of ski goggles he was wearing, "If that's blood all over your hands, then you ain't going to make it out to Parakeet Cay on the back of this ride. That blood ain't coming from no hang nail," Jacob said as he inspected the bleeding wound. Jack was feeling a little woozy, and agreed with him.

"I got a friend-girl who is taking nursing classes. Hang on; we go see her, she be happy to have someone to practice on. Of course, I'll have to charge you, Mon."

Jack had no idea where they were as Jacob raced down back streets and up alleys until they finally came to a full-brake stop in a cloud of coral dust.

"This be Kim's house. You wait here so I make sure she not entertaining nobody."

Jack sat on the back of the moped bent over, semiconscious for what seemed like a long time. He felt hands helping him up and into a small two-room shanty house. Jacob and a woman laid him down gently on the living room floor,

"Jacob, you run down to the store and get a bunch of bandages and anything you can get for infection and bleeding. I got some stuff in my kit but not much. See if Doc Wilson give you some sulfonamide; tell him it's for me," Kim barked out orders like a head nurse in any U.S. hospital.

Before Jacob was out the door, Kim was cutting Jack's shirt and pants off to get at the wound,

"Oh my Dear God, Mon. What you been into?" She sat back on her haunches and looked his body over.

Jack would catch a look at himself in a mirror occasionally and marvel that he was still alive. He had old puckered bullet hole scars, a few slash and stab wounds, an area of destroyed burned tissue, and most recently, the wounds from Burr's shots from a couple of weeks ago. One was torn open, and bleeding freely. Jack knew his weakness was due to blood loss more than any new damage, but it still hurt like hell.

"Mmm-mmm-mm, you one beat up street dawg. What y'all do to earn all this pain?" she said, as she plugged up the bleeding hole with gauze. "I got some stuff I been keeping for emergencies I'm going to put in that hole. It going to sting like the devil, but it will heal that wound up quicker than anything from any pharmacy."

"What is it?", he asked, not real keen on having some island poultice shoved into the wound.

"It's special. My mama got it from Oola Dey herself, back when the fields were burning and all those people got burned up bad about ten years ago. It should still be good, although I can't promise, but it's worth a try. If it doesn't work, we'll throw sulfonamide on it tomorrow."

"Oola Dey? She any kin to Mama Dey, over in Key West?"

Kim jumped back, as if he had slapped her,

"How you know that name? What business you got with Mama Dey?" Kim asked with a mix of awe and doubt, and maybe a tinge of fear. "Who are you, whitey mon? You come in my house with blood dripping, look like you been killed a dozen times, talking about stuff white folks don't know nothing about." As Kim said this, she backed away from him, pulled a crucifix down from the wall over the front door jam, and held it in front of her as if he were count Dracula looking for dinner.

"Take it easy, Mama and I are friends. She helped me when I was sick and I had no one else to turn to. She and I are also mixed up in some bazaar spiritual thing. All tied to some Posse Dude named Jacques Lapin; it's all somewhat confusing. In fact, I need to get in touch with Mama to tell her about Claire and that she needs her help. Plus, she needs to know there are more people coming down with the blood fever...."

"Shut up! I don't want to hear no more of your nonsense. You in shock, done lost too much blood. You talking crazy talk," she spat out.

"What's this all about?" Jacob asked, as he sat a plastic bag filled with first aid supplies on the floor.

"This whitey mon talking crazy. He says he knows Mama Dey and that they're friends in Key West." Kim said, kneeling back down and applying a salve out of an old jar.

"I'm telling you the truth. I know Mama Dey very well. I put her on the plane that brought her down here to fight the Baboon, or somebody," Jack declared. "Do you know her nephew, Tyrone Crawford? He came down with her. In fact, she says Tyrone is her secret weapon and that with him the Baboon doesn't stand a chance."

"I don't know any Tyrone Whomsoever," Kim said, as she filled the gaping bullet hole with the noxious smelling gel.

"Maybe you know him by Ty Obi—

Kim froze, her eyes were wide with fear and astonishment. Her mouth dropped open,

"Don't say that name in this house. I don't need no more trouble than I already got. I ain't getting involved in no fight with no spirits, good or bad." Kim's hands were shaking as she wrapped gauze around his waist and taped it off.

"You need to leave my house. That bandage will keep you together until you can get to a doctor, and don't tell nobody about me helping you either. You forget you ever met anybody named Kim," she said as she gathered her medicines, and put them back in her kit.

"As far as I know, you some kind of devil your own self, just acting like a whitey mon here to steal my body. You git going now, and don't look back neither."

Jacob took one look at Jack's bloody clothes lying in a heap where Kim had cut them off,

"Miss Kim, I can't take no whitey mon on my scooter if he ain't got no clothes on. Maybe you got some things you can *sell* him. Something that makes him looks like he belongs here. What you say, girl."

Kim came out of the back room with a bright red wife-beater t-shirt, a pair of old white jeans and handed them to Jacob. "I'm going in the other room until y'all gone. Be quick leaving!"

"How much do I owe you, Kim?" Jack asked.

"Nuthin, just go."

"Don't worry, Kim, I'll work out the cost with the Mon on your behalf and get back to you," Jacob said, as he helped Jack out the door.

Chapter 21

The Security Guard at the gate entrance to the Parakeet Cay Resort held up a stiff arm for Jacob to stop as They pulled off the highway into the entrance.

"And your business be?" asked the starched guard, as he looked them up and down with distaste.

"Hey Yardie, it's me Jacob Kwame. Don't you have eyes? I got me a cash customer and he wants to come in. So I say, Jacob's your man, I get you in. So open up, and be quick about it."

"Ain't no one look like you two coming inside the Parakeet, tonight or any other night, so get your moped turned around and git."

You don't understand. Mr. Jack was being attacked by Jacques Lapin and his Posse. I swooped in and saved him from certain death. I personally counted thirteen shotta's after us, all of them Jacques's Yardies."

"I'll let you pass, but don't linger. I'm not supposed to allow locals on the premises," the guard said as he waved them through.

Jacob pulled his mo-ped around the entrance fountain and under the hotel's cupola.

"What about Sister Oola and Mama Dey? You said you had to get a message to them. For sure Mon, Mama Dey is with Sister Oola, they almost like the same person. You talking to one, you talking ta other. Maybe I go and see if she taking visitors. I tell her my whitey friend, Jack from Key

West, here visiting me, and needs to give her a message. What you say, Jacky Mon? You want Jacob go cross-island, and fetch her a message?"

Jack thought about getting a message to Mama Dey warning her of the blood fever cases spreading in Miami. He also wanted to tell her about Claire being in a coma in the Aventura hospital and that he was here to take down Jacques Lapin. Jack went inside the hotel lobby and asked the concierge for a piece of paper. He quickly wrote out his message, folded it up, and handed it to Jacob.

"Mr. Jack," Jacob whispered, "I'm not sure if they can read or not. Maybe you should tell me secret like and I'll repeat it just as you say." Jacob said a little embarrassed by this admission. "I'm not saying I can't read," he said, "I'm saying maybe *they* can't, you see the difference. Me, I'm fine, I ain't got no problem with reading, and it's just these island people you got to ask yourself about."

"Ok, listen closely." Jack whispered in his ear.

"Yes sir, I will go this very minute, but first I need to ask you to pay me twenty dollars in advance so I can buy some gas for Shakira. She a thirsty girl and this a big island, Mon."

"Shakira? You mean as in…," he shook his hips.

"No, Shakira my mo-ped, I named her after Shakira…." He shook his hips, and laughed. "You all right for a Whitey Mon."

His eyes got big when Jack peeled off two one-hundred dollar bills.

"I'll be back before noon, Yardie."

Jacob disappeared down the hotel drive in a cloud of smoke and a spluttering engine. Shakira had a long ride ahead of her.

Chapter 22

Burr exited the Market Lane two blocks farther down from Queens Street, sure that he had lost his tail. The traffic on Barry Street was not as hectic as Mad Mike forced himself to stroll rather than run. He wanted to run as fast as he could. He was in danger and wanted to clear the area as quickly as possible. A quick inventory of his pockets took only a second. He had his .32 Berretta, his wallet with several hundred dollars in it, and the clothes on his back; everything else was back at the hostel.

'That fucking Marsh, how did he track me here? The asshole should be dead and laying on a slab in Key West. This changes things again. Fuck Preston, the bastard. I'll pop him later. There's no way he's going to keep his mouth shut if things go bad. Marsh is target number one. I need to get rid of him once and for all, or I'll be looking over my shoulder forever.'

Burr flagged down a cab and instructed the old Rasta cabbie to take him to the New Kingston Hilton. He needed a new cover, clothes, and a place to hide out while he tracked

Marsh. Ten minutes later, the cab pulled up to the new fourteen-story Hilton, dropped Mad Mike off, and sped away. A blast of air conditioning chilled Mike as he entered the lobby, spotted the bar, and walked over to it with a big smile on his face, as if he belonged. The place was packed with vacationers from all over the world. A huge Welcome Shriner's banner hung behind the registration desk. Perfect. Mike eased in between two men at the bar that were drunkenly exchanging stories about how they had survived some bullshit war. Mike sized up the man on his left, same build, similar looks, the man even sounded like Mike.

"What you fellas drinking?" Mad Mike asked as he flagged over one of the bartenders, "Set 'em up for me and my two friends here...and bring over that box of Havana cigars." Mike waved a couple of hundred dollar bills to show that he was flush, "You got to have a good smoke if you're going to drink good scotch whiskey, right?"

The two Shriners moved in close to their new best friend. A good night out on the town could blow their vacation plans. They had a big spender in their sights, the party was just beginning. An hour later, the two men were passed out on their feet, slurring their conversations so badly that Mike didn't have a clue to what they were babbling about.

"Come on partner, I'll help you upstairs to your room. What's your room number?"

The drunk, named Claus Kiedle said something incoherent, and handed Mike his room key.

"916? I'm on the 9th floor also. Come on, you need to get to bed. Tomorrow the real party starts, let's go."

Mike saw that the other man to his right was totally passed out with his head down on the bar. He wouldn't remember a thing.

Twenty minutes later Claus Kiedle was dead. Burr had smothered him to death using a plastic laundry bag from the room's closet. The poor man didn't even know he had died. Burr found the maid's service room down the hall, and placed Claus' nude body in the dirty linen hamper, covered him with damp towels, dirty and soiled linens, rode the service elevator down to the basement, rolled the hamper off the elevator, and returned to *his* new room, and a new I.D.

Chapter 23

A deep rumbling thunder woke Jack from a nightmare where he was caught in a wind tunnel trying to hold on as the gale force winds blew his body out horizontally. He was clipped with a safety belt, the kind skyscraper window cleaners are harnessed in. His clip was being held by a woman whose face was blurred, her body swathed in gossamer flowing out, reaching for him, *Jackie, look in the mirror. Who do you see?*

He came upright, not knowing where he was. The wind was blowing the sheers in ghostly billows with pre-dawn light giving them form and unnerving features. It took him a moment to realize he was awake and that a storm was moving in across the bay in sheets of wind and rain. He fell back on the bed breathing the salty sea air, pushing the dream out of his mind. The rain beating on the roof was soothing. A flash of lightning out over the bay followed with a drum roll of thunder was strangely comforting. Jack's mind went to Claire laying in a coma, not knowing what was going to happen. The doctors had said fifty-fifty, just another way of saying, '*I don't have a clue of what's going to happen. We just have to wait and see.*'

Jack could count on one hand the number of times he had fallen in love, always hoping for that magic mojo to flow both ways, but something always wrecked it and he was left holding the pieces. Love, for him was like jumping from the Brooklyn Bridge with a stout bungee cord tied to his ankles and stopping just inches away from slamming into the water. He would suddenly pull back and away to safety. He could always justify the breakups afterwards, but down deep inside, he knew that he really didn't want them to work and would be the one that would wreck it. Jack loved women just as much as every other guy, but he also loved living on the edge, out where it was him against himself, testing, pushing, going for the rush, going up against the odds and coming out alive at the other end of the tube. The meaner and tougher the adversary, the more intense the jolt. It's like the slam you get when you gulp down five or six ounces of cheap bourbon. For a nanosecond, a mini Hiroshima explodes in your stomach, the shock waves expand out in a bright destructive nova that rolls through your body. When it hits your brain, the cells expand instantly and push out sanity and reason and the bright light becomes the new you, morphed to a higher awareness, a feeling so intense that you crave more, more, more …. never enough.

Jack swung out of bed and walked out on the wide thatch-covered veranda, breathing in deep, letting the sea taste fill his body, rain pattered his face and bare chest as he continued down to the beach and waded out into the dark water. Soon he was taking powerful strokes as he swam away from land, free of all thought, just the sea, the earth's real mother from whence we all came. He dove deep, kicking hard, down, down, until his lungs screamed, blackness closing in around his brain, and still he kicked. Just at the porthole between life and death, he swung around and shot up, breaking the surface with such momentum his whole upper body cleared the water. He sucked in huge lungsful of life, laughing loudly, knowing that he had cheated death again, on his terms.

Tom was sitting on the veranda with a carafe of coffee and a basket of sweet rolls and sticky buns when Jack got back. He took a quick hot shower and put on his last set of clothes that he had brought along with him. He made a note to hit a shop somewhere and stock up on basics.

"So buddy of mine, how are the bullet holes this morning?" Tom asked.

"You know, that voodoo herbal goop the nurse stuffed in the open wound last night must have magic healing powers, the damn thing is closed and scabbing over, go figure."

"I was watching you as you came up the beach, Jack, and I have to tell you, there aren't many men alive today that have the scars that you have. You're going to have to change your line of work to something a little less ...demanding, or you ain't going to make it to fifty, Bro."

"Yeah, I hear you. Maybe I'll go into politics, or insurance; what about stock broker?"

"Jack, you don't know diddly-squat about any of those. I was thinking more like a greeter at one of the big box stores, or pizza delivery. I think that's about all your brain can handle after the life you've lived."

The two friends looked up to watch a large figure running across the manicured grounds, trying to get to them without getting soaked.

"Hey, Agent Roberts! Welcome to Casa Marsh," Tom said, as Agent Bobbie Roberts shook herself, grabbed the napkin off Jack's lap, and wiped her face and short hair.

"How is it that every time I see you, Jack, it's raining? What's with that?'

"Jeez, Bobbie, I was thinking it was *you* that brought the bad weather with you, not *me*."

"Hey listen, I want to give you a heads up on what's happening out at the Burke treasure site. We just got word that a Venezuelan ship is sitting right on top of the site and threatening to fight if anyone comes near or attempts to board her. Meanwhile, El Presidente Maduro is reportedly flying up this morning to announce the Burke discovery is now the Maduro discovery and it belongs to Venezuela."

"What was that I just heard?" Austin Burke asked, as he joined the group on the veranda.

"You heard right. All hell is breaking loose all over the Island as word about the gold is spreading." Bobbie said. "Captain Price is flying in as Florida's representative in claiming ownership. I have to meet him at the airport, then babysit him. I wanted you guys to know the latest skinny," Bobby said, as she grabbed a roll, slathered butter on it, jammed it in her mouth, then ran off the way she had come.

"I better hustle out to the *Sea Bird* and get on the horn to see what has been found out about Chandler. And now I can't make contact with my secretary Cara either. What the hell is going on in Houston. Now on top of that that socialist bastard Maduro is trying to get his gold back. That treasure is mine and I'll be damned if I give it up without a fight. I found that gold and I'll be damned if I'll give it up without a fight," Austin said, and trotted off towards his bungalow.

"Well, amigo, it looks like you and I have the day off. Everything going on has nothing to do with us, I say we charter a boat and go catch some big ones."

"Tom, you have to start taking all this a lot more serious. We are up to our necks in everything going on around here," Jack said pointedly. "Mad Mike Burr is out there, probably close by waiting to kill you and me." Jack paused looking off in the distance. "That fuck is going down hard for Claire, Tommy." Jack sat flexing his knuckles for a moment then continued.

"Jacques Lapin and his DaDa Posse are still a major threat to us, too. Remember he's that asshole that tried to infect me with that juju crap in the bottle, and Mama Dey is here trying to find the source of the Ebola outbreak…."

"Hold on Jack, except for Burr, the rest is none of our business. We stepped up and helped Austin when he needed help. If he wants to go to war with Venezuela that's on him. We didn't sign up to get killed by an RPG. It's even bigger than that now. You heard Bobbie. Bill Price has been sent down here by that nutcase governor of ours to claim the gold. Hell, let him and Maduro duke it out. It ain't our fight. As for the Ebola, man that needs to be under CDC's watch. The more I think about it, I say we haul ass out of Jamaica on the next flight, while we still have our scalps. We're done here. Like old Dug-out Doug Macarthur said, "These proceedings are closed."

"Not yet, Tom, I can *feel* Burr, he's close. I can't leave while he's still breathing. He's here to kill Austin, you, me, and anyone else involved in the treasure. Burr told Austin as much when he had him in that Houston motel before he escaped. Burr was also stupid enough to tell Austin that he was hired by his old nemesis, Wade Preston, to kill him and everyone on the *Sea Bird*."

"Yeah, you're right, I got us into this mess so I need to stick around to help clean it up."

"Let's get dressed and go find Burr. What do you say?" Jack pushed back from the table.

"Let's do it."

Chapter 24

Shakira was smoking and gasping as Jacob pulled into a roadside bodega outside of Ocho Rio. He pulled the spark plug wire to kill Shakira's motor, then sat exhausted from the all-night ride to get to Oola Dey's small cabin. Jacob's body continued vibrating even though the moped was turned off. The coast road had taken much longer, but was much safer than taking mountain roads. Jacob didn't like the mountains at night, He was a city boy and didn't want any part of what goes on up in those mountains after dark. Too many stories about things swooping down from trees, and things walking alongside the road one minute, the next they aren't there. No sir, not for this Yardie.

"Fry me up two of those egg sandwiches with extra onion and plantains on the side. Sprinkle lots of brown sugar on them, too, don't be taking no shortcuts, girl" Jacob ordered from the woman who looked like she was still asleep.

"Mmm hmm, Coffee?"

"Naw, I'll take a cold mango juice. Say, how much farther to Pink Beach cut off?"

The woman swung around from the small butane stove, "Why you want to know that?"

"Cause that's where I'm going, girl, why else you think I would ask," Jacob said as he thought, *'these country folks ain't too bright.'*

"I mean, it ain't none of my business, and I'm just saying like, why you want to go out there? I mean, I don't know myself, but I heard there's some strange goings on out that way. Regular folks shying away from there. Even the lobster men staying off shore."

"What you saying, girl? I been riding all night to get out to Sister Oola's place to give her that very message. There's trouble all over the Island. Ever since they found that gold what's going to make us rich, there's been trouble."

"What gold? What rich? I ain't heard no such thing, but I tell you what, you had better stay clear of that woman. She'll throw a woo-woo on you in a minute, and that be the end of you. Next time I see that moped, it be driving a zombie around."

"Hush girl, you giving me the chills. Hurry up with those sandwiches. I got to be back round the Island by noon," Jacob said, and peeled off a twenty-dollar bill.

"I ain't got that kind of change, Mon, you crazy. That's my whole day's selling."

Same thing happened last night, when Jacob stopped to fill up Shakira. She only holds nine liters and the one-pump station owner had to go around getting change for one of the hundreds Marsh had given him. The guy came back with three twenties and said that was the best he could do. *'Forty dollars for nine liters, fucking country people. Next time, Jack has to pay me in ones.'*

"Keep it, girl. All that news you gave me is worth it. I'll be sure and have my antennas up, and if you see Shakira buzzing back by here in an hour or so, and I ain't on her, call the constable."

The woman stabbed two fingers at Jacob, "Respect Mon, respect. It ain't all about what we see, there's some things we ain't meant to see."

An overgrown crushed-shell road on Jacob's left side caught his attention as he whizzed by it, and he double-backed. *'This has to be it, I don't know how I know that, but I can feel something pulling me.'* Shakira dodged the ruts and pits in the road's shell surface as Jacob's head swiveled back and forth searching the jungle brush for trouble. Something ahead caught his attention and he threw on the brakes. Goose bumps ran circles around his body, his scalp tingled, his mouth puckered as the moisture disappeared. Off in the bushes ahead he thought he saw a tall skinny black man with a blanket over his shoulder. He rubbed his eyes and the image was gone. He goosed Shakira's throttle and sped as fast as she would go down the rutted road. The front wheel hit a pothole and flipped, sending Jacob through the air and crashing into a gumbo-limbo tree.

When he came to, he was sitting on the front porch of a small cabin with a tin roof overhang. A ratty three-legged dog sat at his feet staring at him.

"What y'all staring at? Where is everybody? I need to see Sister Oola and Mama Dey. I got a message for them," Jacob said to the dog.

Surprisingly, the dog trotted off, listing to starboard as he went. A minute later, an old woman with a million wrinkles on her face wearing wire-rimmed spectacles perched on her nose came out of the cabin,

"I'm Mama Dey. You have a message for me from Jack?"

Jacob pulled the folded paper out of his shirt pocket and unfolded it. He had read it several times during the night and had it almost memorized word for word.

"Yes, ma'am, I sure do. I been driving all night to get here. Now, I know y'all don't probably know how to read so I'll just say it out loud. You stop me if you don't understand any part of it."

Mama Dey wanted to thump the boy a good one for implying she couldn't read, but she let it pass.

"Go ahead son, I'll try to keep up."

"Yes, Ma'am." Jacob began reading from the message flimsy,

'Jack said to tell you that the blood fever is spreading in Miami, that's number one. Number two is that Claire is in a coma and paralyzed from a gunshot wound from a man named Mad Mike Burr. Burr is part of the scheme to steal

the gold, kill Jack, and the man that discovered the treasure. And number three, Jack believes that Jacques Lapin is the man behind bringing the Ebola to the Islands. He tried to infect Jack with it in Key West. Jacques DaDa knew that Jack was helping to hide the location of the gold. DaDa got the true location from a crewmember off the boat that discovered the gold. He got him drugged on ganja and then killed him.'

"*That* man was Lamont Troupe, he's my third cousin, his mama Ritha, is my auntie." Jacob said in closing.

"That was a mouthful, Jacob. You got anymore to spit out?" Mama asked.

"No Ma'am, that's all. I'm supposed to ask you what you know and take the message back to Jack. I'm his employee here in Jamaica, and he relies on me to communicate with the locals."

"Do say," Mama said. "Hold my hand, young man."

A while later, Jacob pulled into the same bodega he had stopped at for breakfast.

"I need an ice cold soda, please."

"Well, y'alls back all in one piece. What did you see?"

"Nothing, I couldn't even find the place. I'm heading back around the Island just as soon as I finish off this drink."

Shakira was running hot. A trail of blue smoke followed her as Jacob took the curves and passed slow moving trucks and cars. He was bent forward, goggles down, his watermelon hat flapping in the slipstream. He did not know why he was taking so many chances on the dangerous mountainous roads, all he knew is that he had to see Jack with something to tell him. He couldn't quite put his finger on it, but he knew it would come to him when he met with Jack.

Chapter 25

At the end of Pink Beach Road, Oola Dey's small cabin was quiet. The usual sounds of birds singing, dogs barking off on the beach, and children playing and swimming in the surf were missing today. The wind coming off the northeast shore carried the sound of the breaking surf up to the still cabin, softly blowing the sackcloth curtains. The wind kept the small rooms cool.

"I think the worst is over, Sister Oola," Mama Dey said, as she stood over the huge prone body of Jacques Lapin's mother, Sister Dorothea.

The large woman was lying on a thin mat, hands at her sides, snoring peacefully. A closer look at her black skin showed deep purple-blue bruising over most of her body. Her eyes were swollen and her nose was off center, broken for sure. A front tooth was missing, leaving a gold one next to the new gap. Snatches of hair left several bald spots on the woman's scalp.

The possessed woman had been through a terrible ordeal during the night as the *Baboon* took out his rage on his host's body, slamming her against the container's walls and forcing her to beat herself before he made the jump to Ty Obi. Sister Dorothea was in a deep coma, induced by herbs and ancient prayers the two old conjurers had fed her immediately after pulling her out of the container, as Ty Obi went in and the igloo locked behind him.

The unknown was how much mental damage the *Baboon* had done during his rage. In some cases of evil spirit exorcisms, the host may never wake up, or if she does, she may be an imbecile with no memory; just a blank page for the rest of her life.

"Let's go ahead and put her under the healing blanket," Oola said, as she unrolled an ancient woven reed blanket and set it aside.

Mama Dey brought in several dozen super-heated smooth stones and placed them in small woven bags of herbs and secret concoctions, then placed them around Sister Dorothea's body. She then laid small branches from the gumbo-limbo tree on top of the sleeping woman. Finally, the ancient woven blanket was placed on her, held down by stones.

"That's all we can do Mama. Now we just need to sit and watch. Let her sweat the poison out."

"I'm going outback to check on Ty Obi. It's too quiet, ain't no telling who, or what's inside that contraption with him."

The three-legged dog was sitting alert in front of the container's door. His ears were ticking one way, then another, his nostrils were flared back probing for danger. Mama Dey leaned into the hatch and put her ear against the hot metal, listening intently.

"Nkisi? Mpendla?" Dark One? Death?" Mama yelled out, as she slammed her hand on the door, "Ty Obi?" Nothing, not a sound. The dog stood, sniffed the door, whimpered, and scratched at the coral scrabble to get inside.

A cold chill ran up Mama's back as she wrestled with the decision to open the door or to leave it be for a while longer. Her curiosity overcame her fear, and she threw back the deadbolt, swinging the door wide. The heated stench was awful. Mama gagged when she saw Ty Obi lying on the floor, smeared with feces and blood.

"Oh my God, Child! What did that Devil do to you?" she said, as she knelt beside Tyrone.

He was gasping for air and crying. His arms were swinging wildly fighting off an unseen foe. Tyrone's eyes were unseeing in a mix of terror and horror, the tip of his tongue had been bitten off, his fingernails were broken and bloody, his stomach a mass of deep scratches as if he had tried to disembowel himself.

"Oola, Oola come quick. Help me with Ty Obi."

"Oh *Moganga Nganga,* Benevolent Diviner. Are we too late?"

"*No!* Quick, let's get him inside."

The two tiny women pulled Tyrone by his hands into the small kitchen and immediately started applying ointments, herbal mixes, salves, potent liquid drinks. Loving hands wiped his body off, *Mbula* juju fetishes of every description were draped across his body. Chants and ancient oaths were recited from memory.

Mama Dey sensed something and stopped with a questioning look. A ghostly chorus of voices came from the backyard by the container. She stole a look out the window. Four aberrations were shimmering in the heat by the surf's edge. She saw tall thin men in red robes wavering, seen, but not seen, spears up in salutation, regal in appearance. One moment there was watery form to the figures, the next, wisps of color.

"*Suypa Nini Obi, El Kim Batisho Mpenda, Takuena Nini, Takuena*"

"*Rejoice Mother, the blue monkey is gone. Farewell little mother, farewell*"

The aberrations turned, chanting as they went,

"*OOOLALA-MM, OOOLALA-MM, OOOLALA-MM....*"

The singing faded as they turned, the shapes were swallowed by the bright sun, and then they were gone.

The holy woman squinted and leaned forward as if to ask if what she just witnessed was real or just a trick of the mind. She said a quick *Mbula* prayer, knowing what she had witnessed was real. Her faith was based on millennium of ancestral teachings and spiritual guidance from the very bosom of time itself, *Nsari,* the river that swallows all rivers. The literal translation of *Nsari* in the ancient Bakongo language is, "*In the Beginning.*" The old Shaman returned to her task in deep reflection and prayer. The worse was over, good had won out over evil. The Blue Monkey was gone.

Chapter 26

Jack and Tom were in the lobby of the Parakeet Resort when Jacob skid to a stop under the portico. Jack was talking with Bobbie on his cell. She called to tell him that she and Captain Price were just inside the doors of the Interior Ministry's offices when she spotted Burr across the plaza watching the ministry. Jack told her he was on his way when he watched Jacob skid to a stop at the hotel entrance.

Jacob spotted Jack, pulled the sparkplug wire, and hurried inside.

"Boss Mon, I have a secret for you from Mama Dey, but first you must tell me what it was that she gave to you to protect you before you left her house that last night in Key West."

"Jacob, what the fuck have you been drinking, man? What's with the question?"

"Boss, she said you must tell me, so I can give you the message, that's all I know."

"She gave me a hair and string ball with a grain of sand inside...."

Before Jack could finish, Jacob started talking in a monotone, his eyes were closed, as if in a deep trance.

"Ty Obi is alive, but we may lose him if he doesn't come around in the next several hours. Sister Dorothea, Jacques Lapin's mother is alive and free of the Baboon. I am afraid she will not come out from under her spell, we will just have to wait. In the night, we learned many things from Dorothea, Ty Obi, and the Baboon himself. The people of Haiti, the Dominican Republic, Puerto Rico, Cuba, and Jamaica are in great danger from the blood fever that will be spread by Jacques Lapin if he is not given the gold the whitey mon discovered. Jacques Lapin has sent infected baboon carcasses to each of these Islands. They are in the hands of his people. They have orders to grind the carcasses into pulpy mush, put it plastic bags, and then toss the bags into all the fresh water reservoirs. He must be stopped, Jack." Jacob stopped for a moment, as if changing from low gear into high.

"Someone close to you will be killed today. I don't know who it is, or how it will happen, I just see blood around you," Jacob paused and belched loudly then continued, *"I cannot find Claire. Something is blocking me from her. I see a man in white who is sad standing over her, talking to his God,"* an even louder belch from Jacob startled Jack.

"I must stay here with Oola Dey until we see what happens with Ty Obi and Sister Dorothea. Jack, you are on your own. I cannot help you anymore with my... Shine. You will have to do it on your own. The key is Jacques Lapin. He thinks he has the power of the baboon behind him, but the baboon is gone. Get him Jack, and kill him." Jacob had been standing stiff with hands clenched as he recited his message. He suddenly collapsed to the tiled lobby floor, and sat rubbing his temples, yawning, with a blank look on his face.

Chapter 27

It would be a clear head shot if Jack had an M16 or an AK, but for his Walther, the distance was too great. Burr was leaning against a wall across the Plaza, partially shadowed by a shop's awning

"Bobby, he is about twenty meters to your left, under the awning. I am going to cut straight across the Plaza through the crowds. I hope that I can get on top of him before he realizes what's happening. You edge in and be ready.

"Roger."

Jack pulled the ball cap down low across his eyes and hunched over a bit as he elbowed his way through the noisy crowds of tourists and hawkers. He peeked up on his tiptoes to get his bearings, Burr was gone.

"Bobby, do you see him?"

"Negative, he just melted back into the shadows. I'm about five feet from the storefront and I can't see him."

"Stay where you are, I'm coming," Jack answered, as he pushed his way through the crowd.

Bobby and Jack reached the storefront at the same time. Empty. A woman's body lay behind a small counter, her throat was cut. Jack ran to the back of the store and up a flight of stairs. Bobby pounding up right behind him. On the second landing, a small child sat in front of a TV watching a cartoon. The kid pointed to a closed door and went back to his program. Jack paused at the door and two-handed his pistol.

"Burr? I got you man, you're not leaving that room alive...."

He kicked the door in and rushed in. The room was empty. An overhead hatch in the ceiling was open. Jack scurried up the ladder attached to the wall.

Burr was crouched low running towards Jack. They popped off rounds at the same time. Jack ducked below the hatch, expecting Burr to stick his head over the edge. He waited a few seconds and popped back up. Burr was on the far edge of the roof. He turned and saw Jack, He snapped off a quick shot and jumped. Jack went over the ledge right behind him and landed among a gaggle of tourists trying to get away from the men with guns falling on them. Those close by saw his pistol and went wild trying to get away, trampling their friends in the process.

Jack looked right and left trying to spot Burr. He knew Mad Mike had to be moving with the scared tourists moving away from the square, and joined the flow.

"You just don't give up do you, Marsh?" a voice whispered in Jack's ear, as something cold touched his neck.

"Is that you, Mad Mike?" he asked, as he stopped and let the river of tourists' stream around them.

"The one and only. Turn into that door on your left. I don't want these idiots to be splattered with your blood."

Jack turned the knob on the wooden door and pushed it open. His mind was blank; he didn't have a plan or a clue of what to do next. He knew that the next few seconds were his last. *Mama Dey was right; she saw blood all around. Yeah, his.*

A huge black flash knocked Jack backwards into Burr. They both went tumbling down on their backs in the alley. A Doberman had his teeth in Jack's forearm trying to strip the flesh off. Burr held the gun to the dog's head. Before he could fire, the dog clamped down on his hand. The gun went spinning down the alley.

Jack jumped up, looking for his pistol, lost in the confusion. The dog was doing an awful lot of damage to Burr's arm. Jack could see tendon and bone. Mad Mike was screaming in agony.

Jack kicked Burr as hard as he could in the crotch, then searched around for his pistol. He spotted it just inside the doorway. As he grabbed for it, a black hand snatched it up and pointed it at Jack's head.

"You git, whitey mon, and take that other one with you," an old man said, as he gave a hand command for the dog to back off. The dog straddled Burr, watching him as he rolled in pain, holding his destroyed arm.

Jack aimed a hard kick at Burr's head to knock him out. As his leg started forward, a long bladed knife appeared in Burr's good hand. The knife blade slid through Jack's calf muscle. A quick flick of Mad Mike's hand and the blade sliced out. Blood sprayed over the alley. Another inch and he would have severed a tendon.

Jack grabbed Burr's hand and twisted, trying to break his grip on the knife. He dug the fingers of his other hand into Burr's eyes. Suddenly, a shot was fired that ricocheted off the pavement. The old man pointed the pistol at them.

"You, go that way." He pointed at Jack with the pistol.

"You go the other way. Take your killing away from my house. NOW!" He fired another round into the street.

"I'm going to kill you, Burr," Jack called out, as he limped down the alley.

"Soon Marsh, soon," Mad Mike called from the other way, holding his crotch with his good hand. His bloody damaged hand was tucked up under his armpit.

Jack spotted a Pharmacia across the Plaza and limped over to it. Inside, a man in a doctor's lab jacket spotted him limping and came to him with concern on his friendly face,

"My, my, what have we here," he clucked, as he led Jack to a chair.

He called out to someone in the back and an older woman dressed in a starched nurse's outfit came running over.

"Mrs. Phillips, bring my medical kit along with a pan of hot water, please," he said gently.

Within moments, the nurse was back with the kit. The doctor cleaned the cut and started stitching up the nasty wound. The only painkiller he used was a topical salve that didn't do a thing to cut down on the pain. Jack winced each time he pierced the flesh and pulled the suture tight.

The Doctor looked up at him with a smile, "Hurts, doesn't it?"

"Yes," he said through gritted teeth.

"It's supposed to. This way, you will remember the pain the next time you get yourself in a fix. Are you part of that shooting outside?"

"No, I was in the crowd and was knocked down when everyone started to panic. I got cut somehow."

"Mmm hmm," he said disbelievingly. "That how you got all that blood running down the front of your pants?"

Jack looked down, his pants were soaked with blood. The entrance wound on his waist had opened and was bleeding freely.

"Let me take a look at that." The doctor studied the wound for a minute, then had Jack turn around as he inspected the exit wound.

"Looks like you know somebody that knows *Bush* Medicine. The ingredients for that salve only comes from one place, and I suspect you've never been there, yourself, so somebody fixed you up."

"It's a long story Doc. Can you sew me up in front to stop this bleeding? But this time deaden the area first, please."

"Lay down across those two chairs," he commanded.

Jack felt a pin prick around the wound and then nothing. He could feel pressure, tugging and pulling, but no pain. Soon, he was wrapped in gauze and taped tight around the waist. He was given a shot of antibiotics and a bottle of painkillers.

"Doctor, I really appreciate all of this. I just need to take it easy and let some of these heal instead of running around like a kid," Jack said, reaching for his wallet. "How much do I owe you, Doc?'

The old man laughed politely, "Thank you for the compliment, but I am not a doctor. I am the pharmacia manager. We usually refer sick patients to Doctor Cordoba, but he is on home leave in Havana. As for the money, please, you decide what it is worth to you. The materials, the shot, and pain pills come to U.S. $18.00, say another twenty for Mrs. Phillips and me and we will be happy."

Jack saw that he was serious and not joking and began to laugh. He couldn't help himself. He laughed until his side hurt.

"You are the best doctor I have had in a long time, Sir. Here take this as a show of my appreciation for such a fine job." Jack handed him three one-hundred dollar bills. He would have given him more, but that cleaned him out.

Both the *Doctor* and the *Nurse were* smiling as he limped out.

"Drink plenty of liquids," the manager called out

Jack was still laughing at the absurdity of the events that followed him. The memory of his visit to the Pharmacia would go down in Marsh lore, if he lived long enough to have lore.

He spotted Bobby hustling towards him from a group of local cops. She was red faced and huffing and puffing like a cape buffalo

"Never, ever, jump off a roof again without telling me what you're doing, *Partner*. By the time I hit the roof, no Jack, no Burr, no nada, just me and a hundred TV antennas." She was steaming mad, heat waves rolled off her like hot asphalt on a summer day.

"We're through, Jack. This last stupid move of yours closes the book on us. You want to get yourself killed, fine, but not while *I'm* supposed to be watching your back…"

"Ok, ok," Jack said, holding his hands up in surrender. "It's just that things were rolling fast and it's not like I had time to hold a pow-wow; it was me or Burr, he jumped, I jumped, end of story."

"End of story? Bullshit, where is he? Don't tell me you let him slip away, Marsh."

"Yeah, mea culpa, he got away, but not before I scrambled his huevos really good," he beamed.

"Scrambled huevos don't count, Ace. This guy shot Captain Price. Where is he?"

Suddenly Jack was exhausted. Tired of all the fighting, the pain, and the insanity of this whole mess he was in. He wanted to just turn around and walk away, let someone else deal with it. All the hocus pocus crap, the lowlifes, being responsible somehow for events he couldn't control, or even understand. *Jeezus, Jack,* pandemic diseases, stolen gold, madmen playing with people's lives….and then there's the *Shine.* The closest thing to the *Shine* he ever came across was taking Pam Anderson home one night after the bars closed and the next morning woke up with Olive Oil's sister in bed with him.

"I know that look, you ain't backing out on me now, Ace," Bobby said.

"I'm going home. I'm through with all this, Bobbie. You and the Feds take over. I'm so far over my head; I can't even smell the rat shit anymore." Jack turned and started back across the Plaza. He waved down a taxi and sank down in the backseat with his eyes closed,

"Parakeet Cay Resort, nice and slow."

"Sure ting, Mon, nice and slow."

Chapter 28

Sharp chirping from the parakeets that lived inside the thatched roof woke Jack from a deep sleep. The evening sun had kissed the western horizon goodnight, leaving a band of pink and yellow behind after a long hot day. The bay was flat except for a school of mullet churning the water off the beach. A couple of the resort attendants were busy folding umbrellas and stacking chairs for the night. Jack heard voices, laughter, and island music coming from the main building. He smelled roasting meat over coals mixed with tropical flowers, and was ravenous. He swung his legs over the edge of the bed and sat up. He hurt everywhere. He stood under a steaming hot shower for fifteen minutes, letting his body soak up the heat, feeling the sore muscles start to relax. Afterwards, he stood in front of the mirror inspecting the various cuts and punctures to make sure everything was holding together. The stitches in his calf and the front gunshot wound were zipped tight. The wound packed with *Bush* medicine was looking beautiful and holding together. As he toweled off, he remembered he didn't have another change of clothes. He threw on the robe behind the bath door and padded over to the main building. His target was the resort's clothing and gift shop. He wanted to discreetly get in and out, without attracting attention.

As he walked out from the entrance portico, he spotted Jacob Kwame heading his way.

"Boss Mon, I have a gift for you.'

"Hang loose for a few minutes. I need to hit the gift shop.

"Sure ting, I'll wait under that gumbo limbo tree over there where I got Shakira chained up. Too many tourists around, I can't take no chances."

Jack chose a pair of nice tropical slacks, a low key Tommy Bahama shirt with a parrot pattern, and a pair of sandals. He charged it to his room and dressed in the dressing room

Outside, he saw Jacob where he said he would be and ambled over to him thinking of a nice juicy steak for dinner.

"So, what kind of gift do you have for me, Jacob?" Jack asked smiling at his friend and coconspirator.

Jacob winked and smiled. "Jack I am your managing director here in the Islands, am I not?"

Jack laughed, "Sure, and Executive V.P. of Transportation too, if you want."

"I am more than that, my whitey mon. I am the best private detective in all of Jamaica. I have found something that belongs to you, Jack. Come see."

Jacob led Jack to a dark Ford utility van parked in the shadows against a hedgerow of sea grape. Jack saw the glow of a cigarette in the driver's seat as they approached the van and felt naked without his gun. The side utility door slid open, and Jacob jumped in with Jack right behind him, he stuck his foot against the door track in case he had to beat feet.

A beam from a mag light centered on a pitiful figure, nose broken, eyes swollen shut, lips cut up from broken teeth. The man's hands and feet had zip-lock strips pulled tight, cutting off circulation, swollen and dark.

"Jack, let me introduce you to Mr. Wade Preston. I think you wanted to meet him in person."

Jack was visibly surprised. "Where did you find him? How did you know he even existed…"?

Jacob beamed, "You think I just drive around on Shakira all day talking trash. No. You say I am your employee and Jacob takes that serious. When you were sleeping the other night, I talked with Captain Burke. He told me everything that happened out there on the Blue and about how some of his friends, and some of your friends, were in danger from this man and that I should keep an eye on you in case some bad people try to hurt you or Mr. Tom. So I did some thinking and said why wait for this bad boy to come around. I said to myself, why not go get him and bring this to an end. So here we are."

"Jacob, I'm promoting you to Managing Director of Jamaica. You did good, my friend. Now leave me alone for a few minutes, I need to talk to him privately."

Jack dropped the smile as he turned to the lump on the van bed.

"Preston, you alive?"

"Barely. Thank God those savages are gone, cut me loose here, I've lost all feeling in my hands and feet," he mumbled, spitting blood.

"Uh, uh, not so fast, Hombre. You don't know who I am, do you?"

"You're an American, that's all I need to know, now cut me loose."

"My name is Jack Marsh, asshole. I'm one of the guys you hired Mad Mike Burr to kill, along with a few other people. You're going to pay big time for that." Jack lashed out with a kick. "But you know what *really* pisses me off? Because of you, a woman was shot. She's lying unconscious and paralyzed in Miami and I *really* like that woman. I mean, I like her enough that I would love to run a knife under your skin and start peeling it off, very slow. Maybe do an arm at a time, then a leg, do your face last," Jack said, reveling in the horror of his thoughts.

He kicked Preston in the chest as he slid the door open then closed it behind him and started back to his bungalow. He was in a quandary over what to do with Preston. In honesty, he did want to kill him, but he knew he couldn't. He hadn't fallen that far yet, or had he?

He punched in Burke's cell number. "Austin, this is Jack. I have your old friend Wade Preston with me at the resort."

"Preston, that S.O.B. What's he doing here? I'll be there in thirty minutes, we'll settle this once and for all," Austin said.

"Hold on. I have a better idea. Send Tiny ashore with one of your deckhands to get Preston. Lock him aboard the *Sea Bird* for safe keeping. I want to try and lure Mad Mike Burr out to the *Sea Bird*. Once we have them both aboard, we'll decide what to do with them."

"Roger that. Good thinking, Jack. Tiny's on his way."

As soon as Jack clicked off, the cell rang.

"Jack, this is Mama Dey. We got big trouble. That madman Jacques Lapin sweet-talked his way out of that cage we had him in, saying he was thirsty and was going to die if we didn't give him some food and water. We let him out and that black dog took his Momma and Sister Oola prisoner and headed out for his Momma's house up in the mountains. He said if he's going to die from the blood fever, so are a lot of other folks..."

"Slow down, Mama Dey," Jack said. "Now tell me how he got out of the cargo container."

"He was moaning and begging for water. Sister Oola felt sorry for him and fixed him up a big pitcher of ice water. When she opened the door, he bonked her in the head and run off. He came back a few minutes later driving a car with some woman who he hijacked it from. Then he got his momma in the car, then went around back and trussed up Oola and put her in the trunk. Then he took a stick and hit that lady what owned the car in the head and left her out front under that big gumbo limbo."

"Ok, Mama, I get the picture. Are you ok? How about Ty Obi, I mean Tyrone, is he …back?"

"Naw, he's still over yonder. I can't leave him over there too long, or I won't be able to fetch him back. I don't know how to explain it. I was on the other side with Ty Obi, but I could also see what Jacques was doing. So I come back to hunt you down to tell you."

"How long ago did all this happen?"

"About an hour ago, I had to walk up here to the store to use their phone. Jack, you need to get up there and stop that boy and get Sister Oola back. Sister Dorothea, she ain't coming back, the Baboon had her too long, and she mindless now."

"OK, I'll get it done, Mama, don't you worry. Everything will be ok. I'll let you know when it's over."

"I'll know, Jack, I'll know, you just get it done, son."

Chapter 29

It was after four in the afternoon by the time Jacob pulled the van over and parked a quarter of a mile from Dorothea Lapin's small house in the mountains. The valleys were cloaked in twilight casting gloomy shadows under the jungle canopy that tunneled the road. Colorful birds flitted about overhead seeking a safe haven from the approaching night. A young boy led a swaybacked horse loaded down with burlap sacks filled with coffee beans, both horse and boy looked ready to head for the barn. If Jack didn't know of the danger up the road, he would have found the scene comforting, the end to another day in island life.

His plan was for Bobbie and him to sneak up on the house, find Sister Oola, get Jacques in his sights and pop him from a distance. Jack had no desire to get close to the man and run the chance of getting splattered with any of Jacques's infected blood. From Mama Dey's description, Dorothea Lapin wasn't going to be a problem. She had been exposed to the Blood Fever so she was to be avoided as well. Oola was going to leave with them, blood fever or not. There was no telling what Mama Dey would do to him if he didn't bring Sister Oola back with him. *'Too bad, we don't have that three-legged dog with us.'*

"I don't like sitting out here on this road waiting for y'all to come back," Jacob said, eyeing the overhead canopy and thinking night was coming and the spooky secrets it held. "I think you're going to need me if trouble starts, Jack."

"I need you to stay here and wait for us. When you see us coming you get this van cranked up." Jack said, as he checked the load in his pistol.

Bobby was already out of the van adjusting her shoulder holster and tightening her belt a notch. She was back in her black pantsuit outfit with the white shirt and tie for all the world to see resembling a portly Blues Brother.

"Are you ready?" he asked.

"Yeah, let's go do it."

They walked quickly, taking the path next to the road. They avoided the pot-holed pavement in case some kamikaze mo-ped, or a ganja-head decided to aim for the two whitey mon on their mountain turf. Jack's excitement was starting to build as they got closer to the narrow cut off that led up to Dorothea's house.

Bobbie was in her groove, focused and ready. They cut through a small stand of coconut trees that led to a hedgerow of sweet smelling flowers and berries. Beyond the hedge was Dorothea's house. A dirty four-door Toyota was parked in front, trunk open. The porch was in shadows, but he could see a dim light coming from the back of the house.

Jack nudged Bobbie, indicating for her to wait there as he made a crouching run for the porch. Once safely ducked down by the porch steps, Bobbie slid in next to him. Their weapons were up and ready. Adrenaline was shooting through Jack's veins as he crept up to the screen door, expecting a shotgun blast, or an automatic to rip into him at any second. A floorboard squeaked inside making his heart almost break a rib. He stood in the shadow, his gun hand was steady but inside was doing the funky chicken. He looked over his shoulder, Bobbie was gone, the yard was empty, the hedgerow a smear of shadow among the coming night.

The screen door *screaked* as he pulled it open and stepped inside. He hugged the wall, trigger slack gone, ready to light up the night and run for it. Jack sensed someone else in the room with him, but couldn't pinpoint where they were. His night vision played games with him as objects in the room gave the illusion of being something they weren't. He used a Marine sniper trick of not looking directly at the objects, but out of the corner of his vision. He spotted a figure standing against the wall across the room, motionless. He squatted down slowly and crawled to his right. The figure still didn't move. He crouched low, pistol stiff-armed out in front of him, and walked up to the figure. It was Sister Dorothea.

"She's out of it," Bobbie said at his elbow.

"*Jeezus, Bobbie*! Don't do that, I could have shot you, sneaking around like that." His heartbeat echoing around his skull.

"I came through the kitchen, nada, no DaDa."

Sister Dorothea's eyes were partially rolled back in her head, face slack and expressionless. Jack snapped his fingers a couple of times to make her blink, but nothing happened

She was off in hoodoo land somewhere. Jack backed away from her, pulling Bobbie with him.

"Don't let her breathe, or cough on you, she has the fever," he said.

At that moment, a male voice called out from the back porch.

"*Mére, venir á moi*, Mother, come to me."

Without a moment's hesitation, Dorothea turned to the kitchen door and walked to the sound of the voice. Jack and Bobbie hugged the wall not knowing what to expect. They heard the screen door open, and the creaking of the back porch steps, then it was quiet again.

"This is giving me the creeps," Bobbie whispered.

"Me too. Let's follow them and see what Jacques is up to."

By the time they were on the back porch, Jacques and his mother had disappeared in the dark. The outline of a small shack was off to the left, to the right was a path leading into the dark. Jack signaled Bobbie to stand-fast while he checked out the shack.

As he got closer, he saw that it was a tool shed with a chicken coop attached to it. The acrid tang of fresh chicken droppings was strong. A few clucks and squabbles from the dark made him jump. He turned to backtrack when a sound caught his attention

"Brrrrock, broc, broc, brrroc..."

He knew that cluck wasn't coming from any chicken. The last time he heard that cluck was when Mama Dey was dancing over him to rid him of the baboon's curse, *'Damn Jack, listen to yourself, you're starting to talk this hokey pokey crap.'*

He eased the hammer back on his pistol and slowly pulled the shed door open. His nerve-endings were snapping like live electrodes. The clucking had stopped; inside was as black as a crackhead's future.

"*Cluck, Cluck,*" he said softly.

"I ain't ever heard a chicken say *cluck* like that, so that must be Mr. Jack Marsh coming to rescue me. Is that so?"

"That's so," he answered back, feeling his way to where the voice was coming from. He tripped over something soft.

"Was that you I just stepped on?"

"It was, now get me un-tied and let's scoot before that monster comes back for me. He said he was going to get his momma settled and then he was coming back for me. Let's get out of here, Jack."

"*Bobbie,*" I called in a stage whisper over my shoulder.

"Shhh, I'm right here, Ace," she said at his elbow.

"Damnit, Bobbie, I said don't do that. I swear, the next time, I'm going to unload a knuckle sandwich on that mug of yours."

"A knuckle sandwich? Jack I haven't heard that since I kicked Billy Tippet's ass in high school."

"I'm waiting for someone to notice I'm tied up down here," Sister Oola said tartly. "That madman is going to be back any second."

Oola's hands and feet had been loosely bound and it took less than a minute to untie the knots. Once she was up on her feet they made it across to the front yard.

"Bobbie, take Oola back to the van and wait for me. I'm going back and sit in the shed until Jacques comes back. After that, things will go quickly, and I'll be down that road like a streak."

"Jack, I'm not going to miss out on this. You wait for me, and we'll do it together. Besides, we're going to need an *official* version of what took place, and I'm the *Official*, Ace. We need to try and bring him in alive."

"Alive! *Excuse me!* Did I hear someone say bring him in alive?" Jack said sarcastically, "This guy has the Ebola virus running through him like battery acid, eating him up by the second. Sorry pal, he's not leaving this mountain top. Him or his mother. Now get your ass down the road, like I said."

Bobbie stood, chest puffed out, knuckles popping, staring at him, *Pissed*. She grabbed Oola's hand and led her off into the dark.

"If I'm not at the van in thirty minutes, haul ass out of here," he called to the shadows melting into the night.

On a hunch, he crossed the backyard and squatted by the path leading off into the dark. A light rain had started falling, masking any warning sounds. The night air and rain were chilly. Jack shivered as his head and back soaked up the rain. The thin material of the gift shop shirt did little to repel the rain or mask his musky sweat smell. Anyone coming up the trail would smell him if they were alert. He let his thoughts wander and began to doze. The long days and nights with little sleep and the constant danger were taking their toll on him.

Jack snapped awake as a shape walked right past him. He could have reached out and touched it. He got up slowly. His legs were cramped from squatting and followed the figure. He raised his pistol, aiming at center mass.

"Jacques?" he said, planning to shoot the moment he turned around.

There was no response as the figure kept walking towards the house. He realized it was Sister Dorothea still in her trance, plodding flatfooted back to her house, and up the porch steps. Jack stood at the bottom of the steps and watched her sit in a straight-backed kitchen chair, hands in her lap, eyes rolled back, expressionless.

Jack backed away, turned, and headed for the path. The rain was coming down hard now, making the clay path slippery. He followed it for about a hundred yards when it opened into a clearing. The clearing had a fire pit in the center with a palm-frond hut on the far side.

He stayed in the undergrowth as he worked his way around to the back of the hut. He pulled back a woven reed window covering and spotted Jacques lying on a matt with a candle lit at his head. His torso was soaked in blood. He was naked except for a pair of bloody shorts. There was no doubt that he was in great pain and feverish as he thrashed about. Jack's instinct was to help the man, but the thought of the horrific disease kept him rooted in place.

"Jacques DaDa," Jack called out.

"Who is it? Who is there? Bring me water, hurry," he begged.

"I am sorry my friend, I can't. I might catch the blood fever if I get close to you."

"No, I swear. I am DaDa. I am the nephew of the last King of Scotland, Idi Amin DaDa. I will give you anything you want." He moaned in despair.

"If you tell me where the baboon carcass is, I will give you water and medicine to ease the pain."

"It is a lie. I don't have a carcass. I sent them all to Haiti to be used to kill that island. It is an accursed land. They sold their souls to the Blue Monkey in exchange for freedom from the white man's whip. Look at it, a festered boil upon the earth. There is no place for it in my United Caribbean. I swear this is true."

"I don't believe you, Jacques. Sister Oola told me that you had one carcass hidden here somewhere. I believe her. Tell me where it is and I will put you out of your pain and suffering."

As if on cue, Jacques threw up a gobbet of blood. His body was ulcerating and splitting open before Jack's eyes, like something evil was trying to get out. Bloody snot drained from his nose, he was mad with pain, shaking uncontrollably.

"In the shed, behind the chicken coop is a wooden box, inside is a freezer. The carcass is in it," he pleaded. "Shoot me, please, kill me, make the pain stop...I hurt so...."

BANG!

Jack's shot caught him in the head, killing him instantly.

Jack ran back up the path, slipping a couple of times, rolling in the red clay. Inside the shed, he found the wooden box built to resemble a feed box, or a storage area. Inside was the freezer, no electricity, the top was warm to the touch. Jack ran back to the house and flipped on all the lights he could find. He found an oil lantern and a box of kitchen matches then ran back to the shed.

Inside the shed. he found a couple of buckets and a garden hose. He cut a few feet off the hose to use to siphon gas out of the Toyota. He gagged as he swallowed a mouth full of gasoline as he sucked the hose. Once the buckets were full, he ran back to the clearing lugging one of the sloshing buckets along the path. He threw everything that would burn onto Jacques's body then poured the gasoline over him. Jack fired up a rolled newspaper with a kitchen match and tossed it inside the hut.

'*SWOOSH*!'

The heat roiled out as flames consumed the shack. Jack covered his nose and mouth from the stench of burning hair and skin. He stood and watched for a minute until he was satisfied that the job was being done and then ran back up the path, falling again, getting a mouthful of clay to mix with the taste of gasoline.

He went into the hen house and rousted as many chickens as he could, then flipped open the freezer. Holding his breath, he poured the other bucket of gas over the carcass. He stood back a few yards and tossed in the lit lantern and hauled ass.

Within seconds, the tool shed, hen house, and the freezer were a giant torch lighting up the night. He ran for the road, as the van came skidding up the driveway, horn honking, lights blinking.

"Move it, Jack, we got company right behind us," Bobbie yelled out.

He didn't need any encouragement and made a flying leap into the side door, as Jacob floored the old van. The clunker jumped into life and they fishtailed down the drive and up the highway.

"Wooeee! I smell chicken shit," Sister Oola said with her face scrunched up.

"I don't think that's chicken shit you're smelling, Sister," Jack said straight faced, looking her right in the eye. A moment later they were all laughing uncontrollably, releasing the tension, letting the adrenaline burn off.

Chapter 30

By the time they had everyone showered and bunked down back at the Parakeet it was almost four in the morning. Jack was sitting on the lanai with Tom sharing how the night went down. Jack was anxious about Preston being held prisoner on the *Sea Bird* anchored out in the bay. He watched the dim shape of the trawler as it swung on its anchor line a half mile offshore.

"Austin's staying on the *Sea Bird* with Tiny Miles and his two crewmen. They're taking turns on watch making sure no one comes within a quarter mile of them unnoticed," Tom laughed, "The two crew are the same ones we captured sneaking aboard the *Sea Bird* to kill us last week off Point Royal. The two Rasta's had a serious, "Come to Jesus" moment with us initially and are now devout believers in living a straight life. Of course, that all might change when they hear their leader and mentor, Jacques Lapin, has departed this earth."

"What about Preston? Where is he?"

"Chained to a motor mount in the *Sea Bird*'s engine room. He's not going anywhere."

"Bobby wants me to turn him over to her. She wants to charge him for attempted murder for shooting Captain Price.

"Let's talk this through for a moment, Jack. Is there anything that Preston can point to that could jam us up?" Tom was leaning forward as he spoke. "Have we left any trails, or loose ends? We've had a couple of up-close rumbles and I know there has to be witnesses to some of the action. Can we safely just leave and not have any blowback? Think back, is there anything we did in Key West or Miami that we can be nailed with?"

"This project isn't over yet, Tom. Burr is still alive and out there stalking us. At the moment, he is the biggest threat to us. He is a psychopath, and will kill anyone that gets between him and his target. We need to shoot him on sight, no talk, no bullshit, just one to the brain housing." Jack looked his friend in the eye, and said, "Actually, it would all be cleaned up nicely if Preston were to have an accident on the *Sea Bird*. Maybe falling down a hatch or accidently falling overboard. Like they say, no ticky, no talky."

"Jack. You know we can't pop Preston, don't you? I'm all for protecting ourselves. but we can't just kill the man."

Jack sat back thinking of all the shooting and killing over the past couple of weeks and marveled that more people hadn't been killed or hurt.

"Yeah, I know, talking feels good, but doing it, nah, we can't. I'll turn him over to Bobbie in the morning and let her run with it. I don't think there are any trails leading back to us, but even if there is, it's us against him, and right now his word is for crap."

"I'm thinking that's the smart thing to do. The sooner we can shake off all these crazy people the sooner we can concentrate on bringing the gold up."

"Why don't you catch some z's? I want to sit for a while before I hit the rack," Jack said, standing up, stretching, and yawning big.

Jack stood ankle deep in the surf, looking out at the *Sea Bird,* riding at anchor at the mouth of the bay. Overhead were a billion stars mixed in with a billion more farther out. A shooting star shot across the heavens as a reminder that there is just as much danger out in the cosmos as there is down here on earth. You never knew when a tracer round would come at you at light speed. Jack loved the night, it offered protection, it allowed a man to sneak up on his enemies, or to fade away into the night.

Jack could feel eyes on him as he stood in the shadows. He couldn't tell if they were friendly eyes, or enemy eyes, he just felt them. He scanned the tree line that sat back from the beach, neck hair tingling, reaching out, sensing danger. The coconut and banyan trees were park-like on the resort grounds, but higher up, it became triple canopy jungle. He casually walked in the sand, leaving footprints behind him, on a leisurely stroll, until he came to the edge of the resort property. He quickly walked into the shadows of the canopy and stood behind an ancient coconut tree watching for any movement. The smell was the first indication of something wrong. He closed his eyes tight and focused his hearing 90° to the right, then 90° left, breathing lightly through his nose to catch the scent again. There were night sounds of birds nesting overhead and little night-critters scampering around, but the smell was what guided him. He moved from tree to tree, bush to bush. The smell grew stronger as he approached a thicket of brambles and wild palms.

He crouched low to the ground to get a better sight picture by looking up into the night starlight. Ten meters in front of him was a hump on the ground. The closer he got, the more powerful the scent of blood and feces. Ten feet out, he stopped, knelt, listened, and watched. After five minutes, he crawled closer until he was a couple of feet away from the body of one of the resort security guards. He felt for a pulse, his hand came away wet with warm blood, the man's throat had been slashed. Jack pulled in closer to the body, running his hand over the man's chest, feeling for body heat, his hand came away warm and wet with blood.

A chill ran up Jack's spine. Ten minutes ticked by without any unusual sounds. He decided to make a run for it. He ran in a crouch, moving quickly through the coconut grove, then back to the bungalows. Standing in the shadows of the lanai, he watched for any movement. Nada, the night was still except for the breeze rustling the palm fronds.

Chapter 31

Off in the tree line, Mad Mike watched Jack settle down in a lounge chair on the lanai to stand guard. A half hour earlier, Burr had been standing in the shadows near Jack's bungalow listening to the two men talk. Mad Mike's plan was to kill Marsh, Parker, and Burke and then scoot. When he heard the two men discuss killing Preston themselves, Burr smiled, thinking how much the three of them were alike. The best news though was that Preston was on the *Sea Bird Explorer*, not more than five hundred yards offshore, chained up in the engine room. Mad Mike got an erection thinking of having all three of his targets so close and how much he was going to enjoy killing each one.

When Jack had started for his walk on the beach, Burr had backtracked to the safety of the tree line. He stumbled into the security guard by accident. The dumb little shit had just lit a cigarette ruining his night-vision as Burr stepped up and cut the man's throat. As Jack approached the dead guard, Burr squatted, and watched from fifteen meters off. He was tempted to kill him then, but decided not to, knowing that Preston was a higher priority. Mad Mike had fought the urge to leap out and cut Jack's throat just to watch him die. Once Jack had scurried back to the compound, Burr followed him to make sure that he wasn't going for reinforcements or sound the alarm. The night was quiet as he watched Jack in the shadows. The powerful erotic urge to kill Jack was almost uncontrollable. The blood lust was searing his nerve-endings like arcing electrodes. Mad Mike clamped down on his lower lip, drawing blood. The moment passed, and he slipped back into the shadows, arteries on fire.

Mad Mike popped the small lock on the cabana hut that contained the resorts water equipment and toys. He quickly pulled out a two-man kayak, and within minutes was paddling silently out towards the *Sea Bird*. This time of the morning anyone on watch aboard the *Sea Bird* would be dulled by the boredom, if not asleep. The kayak ran swiftly across the water as Mad Mike put his shoulders into the strokes.

He approached the *Sea Bird* bow-on, grabbing the anchor line to stop his forward motion. The kayak nestled up under the pulpit, as Mad Mike secured a painter-line to a forward cleat. Balancing himself, he stood and pulled himself up onto the forward deck, soundlessly, MP5 ready to rock if necessary. Reggae music was drifting softly from the wheelhouse, the communications equipment on the bridge gave off a soft glow, outlining a man sitting in the captain's chair, chin on chest.

Mad Mike worked his way to a starboard hatch amidships and carefully stepped over the knee-knocker and stood with his eyes closed to adjust his night vision to the near black interior. A ladder to his left led down to below-decks and the engine compartment two levels down. The engine room was lit with a caged red nightlight that gave the room an eerie setting for what Mad Mike had planned. Mike closed and dogged the hatch behind him. It took a few minutes to spot Preston sprawled out on the deck, chained to an engine mount, fast asleep.

"Hey Wade, wake up," Burr said, as he nudged him in the ribs with a booted foot.

"Wha...who...Mike? Thank God. Quick, get me loose from these fucking cables—

"Uh uh, not so fast. I've got a few questions first," Mad Mike said, as he squatted down to keep his voice lower.

"Questions? Get me the fuck loose, I'll answer questions later."

"You fat little fuck, I'll cut you loose when I'm ready," he said, and backhanded Wade across the mouth, "Where is my money, asshole?"

"What are you talking about? What money? I wired you all the money we agreed on."

Mike punched Wade in the nose. Blood splattered across the engine block, "Yeah, you sent it, and then the next day you pulled it back."

"I did no such thing. Why would I do that? I hired you to do a job, and I paid you in full. You fucked it up big time. When I got word of all your fuckups, I came out here to do the job myself. What are you doing now, coming back for more money? Forget about it, I'm not paying another cent.

You've fucked up a simple assignment, so forget about it." Wade's nose was flowing blood down his face onto the deck.

Mad Mike pulled out his folding knife and flicked it open with a snap of his wrist. The long thin blade looked like burnished copper in the red light. He placed the tip against Wade's right eyebrow and applied a little pressure. Blood began to seep out of the small puncture.

"I did this to a woman recently who lied to me. She finally admitted her lie by the time I started on her breasts. On you, I'll skip the breasts, and go straight to the old tamale. Now, tell me where my money is."

"I swear I sent it, Mike, I swear. My word is as good as gold…"

Mad Mike flicked down, cutting through the eye and the cornea. "AAAHH! *Oh my God, ahh! Stop, please, I swear, I'm telling the truth.*" Wade cried out.

Mike held his hand over Wade's mouth, listening for running footsteps, or voices. The *Sea Bird* was over a hundred and thirty feet in length, with thick steel walls to buffer any noise. Someone would have to be standing outside the steel hatch to hear Wade's screams. Mike smiled.

"So, if you are not lying, then who reversed the wire transfer?" Mike asked calmly, as Wade cupped his eye, sobbing.

"You're insane. The prison shrink in Huntsville told me to be careful, that you are crazy, and not to trust you…"

The blade flicked out, catching Wade on the forehead over the other eye.

"Is that what that Doc said? I'm crazy? No, Wade, *I'm* not crazy, I'm fucking *INSANE*," he laughed at his words. "If I could, I would kill everyone on this island, one cut at a time, heh-heh-heh." Mike cackled madly.

He had finally given in to his suppressed cravings, letting the insanity flow over him like an orgasm. No more pretending, no more acting normal, "*Noomoremisternormalguy.*" He screamed, as he began slashing, stabbing, and cutting insanely. Wade tried to fend off the attack, but Mike was in a killing frenzy and Wade couldn't fight back. The slashing became stabbing, deep killing wounds. Wade was dead, but the slaughter continued, the blood lust roaring through Mad Mike's body until finally spent, he fell across his victim, exhausted, sobbing in hatred and loathing.

A while later, Mad Mike gathered himself, looking down on what was once Wade Preston, now just a bloody mess. He felt nothing, empty inside, except for a glimmer of disgust deep down somewhere. He knew he had crossed the line, but didn't care. He knew his life was over, there were no more places to run. Without a stash, he would be broke in a month. Besides, he was probably the most hunted man on earth, even more so than that goatfucker Osama had been over in Turdstan, or wherever. If he gave himself up, he would ride the needle or take the jolt in less than a year. '*What a shitty way to go out.*' No, he was going out on his terms, they weren't going to fry his brains. Another couple of hours and they'll be coming down to take Preston away, that would be his chance.

'I'll take them all out with me, that fat FBI Bitch, the smart ass Burke, and Marsh. Yes, indeedy, Jackie Fucking Marsh, and any others that get in the way, will have to go too.'

Mad Mike un-dogged the engine room hatch, then slipped back inside a gear locker to wait for whoever showed up first, senses lulled by the adrenaline burn off.

Chapter 32

Jack sat peering into the shadows waiting for Burr to come at him. He could sense danger but didn't know where it was coming from. He was tired, his body was burned out from all of the adrenaline that had dumped into it over the last few weeks. He wanted a drink and was tempted to call room service to have a bottle of Jack Daniels delivered to him along with a bucket of crushed ice. He could taste it, he could feel it burning its way down his throat, hitting his stomach in an atomic burst of ethyl alcohol. He shook the vision off and spat to clear the imaginary taste from his mouth. No matter what, he resolved, he would never drink again. Jack was dozing quietly as the thought occurred to him that Burr was going for Preston. He sprang awake and jumped to his feet.

Of course, it had to be Burr that killed the hotel guard. Jack did not believe in coincidence. Too many things had happened to him to know better than to shrug off things that were obviously connected. He grabbed Tom's binoculars off the table and focused on the *Sea Bird*. She was riding quietly on the calm bay. As he moved his vision from right to left he saw the kayak tied off on the bow. It was out of place; it didn't belong there. His hunch was right; Burr was on the *Sea Bird.*

Not wanting to sound an alarm that might warn Burr, Jack ran for the beach hut and pulled a kayak and a paddle from the rack and made for the water. Once in the kayak, he dug deep with the paddle and the little skiff ripped across the water. Twenty yards out from the *Sea Bird,* he shipped the paddle and let it glide in under the bow, tied off on a cleat, and lifted himself aboard.

Jack was hunched down on the pulpit when he spotted a shadow near the forward hatch where the submersible was dogged down. By the shadow's size he knew it wasn't Burr,

"Tiny?" he whispered.

"Yeah, Jack, is that you?"

"Yeah, what's going on?"

"Stinky was on watch and spotted somebody down here on the deck sneaking around. I figure it had to be your mutt coming for Preston. I went down to the engine room to check on Preston, but the hatch had been dogged down from the inside. I stuck my ear to the door and heard muffled screams and then it got quiet. I put a cheater bar across the hatch so whoever is still alive in there is locked in."

"Good work. What about Austin and your crew, where are they?"

"All three are on the bridge. We were just getting ready to send Austin to shore to notify you guys. Stinky and Jody are ready to swim from here to Cuba, to get away from whoever is in the engine room," Tiny laughed.

"Stinky and Jody?"

"Yeah, the two gun monkeys Tom and I beat the crap out of that night off Point Royal. They've turned out to be a couple of good seamen."

"Listen, it's going to get nasty out here. Take Austin and your two guys and head for shore. I'm going to clean up things out here."

"What are you talking about when you say, *clean up?*"

"It means, *clean up.* You don't need to be around for this. It's going to go down fast and the more people aboard the chances someone is going to get hurt. Now, take the kayaks, and get going. I want to do this before the sun is up." Jack said.

The sky was starting to lighten to the east. In another half-hour the sun would be up.

"Before you go, turn off all equipment, lights, generators, all power, shut her down. Can you do that?"

"Sure, and I understand, no witnesses, no problems. Be careful, Jack. I don't know what went on inside that engine room, but it sounded like a wild animal tearing and gnashing. The screaming was coming from a terrified animal."

Tiny hopped up the ladder to the ship's bridge. A few minutes later, Austin and the two deck hands hurried by with Tiny carrying something in his hand.

"Here's a flare gun. If things get out of control, fire it off and I'll be here with reinforcements in a flash."

Austin came back and hugged Jack, "You've got guts. I knew I could count on you when trouble came around. Shoot straight, Jack," and he was gone over the side.

Jack took the flare gun and placed it on the submersible's frame. He had a repugnance for flare guns after he saw what one could to a man. Briar Malone had shot a man in the chest last year aboard the *Island Girl* off St John's who was coming at her. Jack had puked after one look at the dead man.

Jack took a look around, saw the two kayaks with Austin and his crew making for shore. The sky was definitely getting lighter in the east. He drew in a couple of deep salty tasting breaths and started down the starboard side. At the second hatchway, he ducked in, letting his eyes adjust to the dark companionway. He took the ladder down two flights and stood facing the engine room hatch. His heartbeat had picked up noticeably. He breathed through his mouth slowly, trying not to hyperventilate. He put his ear to the hatch and could make out someone singing or humming.

He removed the cheater bar from the hatch handle. The sound of metal on metal was loud enough to warn anyone inside; he didn't care. Standing off to the side, he heaved the hatch open all the way. No gunshots. He stepped inside, letting his eyes adjust to the even darker interior.

"Mad Mike, it's me, I've come for you," he said softly.

"Marsh?"

"The one, and only."

"He-he-he, good. How do you want this to go down? Guns, knives, hands, mine's bigger than yours. You call it."

"How about you just give up, and take the fall for shooting Captain Price and all the innocent people that got in your way?" he asked.

Jack could feel his body begin to hum. Adrenaline was dumping into his veins; his senses were vibrating danger signals. The smell of Preston's blood added to the primal scene.

"I'll bet if you asked for leniency, all those bleeding heart do-gooder judges would just give you a couple of pills that let you go beddy-bye forever. Just close your peepers for eternity," Jack teased, trying to get Burr to move.

"Fuck you, Marsh. I ain't giving up nothing. If you want me, you're going to have to kill me."

Jack focused on where Burr's voice was coming from. He could tell that Mad Mike had moved between taunts. He squatted down, and breathed through his mouth.

"Jackie, where are you, lad? Come closer. I have a present for you."

Something hit the deck three feet in front jack and rolled. He reached out for whatever it was. His hand touched something wet and round, *Preston's head?* Jack jerked his hand back from the mess then reached out, grabbing it by the hair, and tossed it off to the side. It made a dull thud when it hit, but it was enough to spook Burr. Two fast rounds went off, lighting the room for a nano second. Jack saw Mad Mike ten feet to his front, crouched, pointing his weapon off to his right. Jack capped three quick rounds, sure he had hit his mark. The shots deafened him. His ears were ringing and didn't hear Mad Mike until he was on top of him. He felt a deep burn in his shoulder. Jack grabbed Mad Mike's shirt and fell backwards pulling him with him. Jack sprung up, kicked out in the dark, connecting with something. He heard a loud grunt. A gun flash next to his crotch scared him, but missed. Jack kicked out again, hitting air.

The steel plate deck rang out with the sound of running footsteps. A second later, three rounds exploded from the companionway. Jack fired at the general direction of the shots, then it was quiet, graveyard quiet, scared out of your fucking brain quiet....

"Mike?"

"Yesss," Burr answered, in a weird voice, "You cheated Jack... you got lucky.... ya hit me with that peashooter of yours. What ya say we go topside .... get out of the dark so we can watch each other bleed.... huh partner?"

Jack fired his pistol down the companionway in the direction of the voice until the slide locked back on empty. He tossed the pistol aside as he walked towards Burr's voice. He picked up the cheater, a lead pipe about four feet long and began swinging it in big arcs, hoping to catch Mike in the dark.

Jack came to the ladder leading up and saw Burr scurrying into daylight. He was right behind him, climbing faster than any monkey ever climbed. At the top, he came out into a bright sunny day.

Mad Mike was looking off to the shore, not realizing that Jack was behind him. Jack swung at him with all his strength, aiming for the head, but missed and hit his shoulder. He heard the collarbone crunch. Mike went down in pain. Jack slammed him in the gut with the pipe, surely rupturing something. He was determined to beat the man to death.

Burr raised his pistol and fired a round that caught Jack in the hand, blowing off his pinky finger,

"FUCK THAT HURTS!" he screamed in pain.

Jack kicked out and the pistol skittered across the deck and over the side. An instant later, Burr was up with a long thin knife in his hand. Jack grabbed the knife hand and squeezed, pain shot up from his bleeding hand. Mike pulled Jack in close. They were cheek-to-cheek grappling, whiskers scratching each other. Mike bit Jack's nose hard, blood starting flowing. Jack squeezed Mike's nuts with an iron grip with his good hand. Mike screamed, spitting nose blood over them. Jack went for Mike's eyes with his good hand, his thumb finding a sweet spot, and jabbed.

The shock to Mike's eye was too much and he threw himself backwards, taking Jack with him over the side. Hitting the water revitalized them. Jack grabbed Mike's crotch again and squeezed. Mike opened his mouth to scream and gulped in a lung full of saltwater. Jack reversed position and began swimming and kicking deeper. Mike fought like a madman, jerking and flailing his arms to break loose. Jack turned on the power and kicked even harder, pulling Mike with him deeper and deeper, never letting go of his nuts. Somehow, Mad Mike had managed to hold on to his knife and was lashing out. Jack grabbed the knife hand and pulled it free from Mike's grip. Mike was losing consciousness. Jack pulled him in close so he could see his eyes,

"*This is for Claire,*" he screamed incoherently into the water, then slammed the knife blade upward, deep into Mike's chest.

Mad Mike didn't seem to notice at first, then his eyes went wide when the pain hit. He knew he was dead, a mix of hate and shock ran across his face, then an evil sneering grin spread, as if he could read Jack's thoughts.

Jack let go of the body letting it sink and made for the surface. His lungs were raging for oxygen. His vision became pinpricks. He was about to black out just as he broke the surface, then air, life-giving air. He gulped in lungsful as he floated on his back.

Jack floated letting the craziness burn off. He heard an outboard motor from what seemed a long way off, and ignored it. The next moment, Tom and Jacob were pulling him aboard a dingy.

"He's alive! I told y'all not to worry. He's a Double O Agent like me. Take more than some mean-assed crazy man to throw Jack Marsh off his game."

Jack was coughing and spluttering, trying to clear his throat, and gulping in air at the same time. He looked at the three men, never so glad to see such friendly faces in all his life.

Tom was looking at him with a scowl on his face,

"Jackie, Jackie, will you ever listen to your sergeant? Never go out on a patrol without telling someone," then he gave Jack a big hug.

Chapter 33

The sun was setting out over the Western Caribbean, throwing off pinks and rose colored shafts as it dipped below the horizon. The darkening sky overhead was already starting to fill with diamond dots of early evening stars; the surf was a whisper of foamy bubbles, as it made its run up onto the beach. The Parakeet Resort was quiet.

Tom and Jack were sitting on the lanai, feet up, enjoying the evening. The meds the Doc gave Jack took away the pain from the day's battle with Mad Mike. Sometime during the fight, he was stabbed in the shoulder. His hand was wadded up like a beehive, protecting the nub where half of his little finger had been. He didn't know how he was going to get along without his pinky, *'Oh well, there goes another disguise. I was never good at posturing anyway.'*

"Jack, it's time for us to shove off," Tom said, blowing out a huge cloud of smoke. "Our mission here is done. We need to head over to Louisiana and get that recovery boat lined up while Austin argues with the Cubans and the Venezuelans over salvage rights. Seems like neither country has the capability to lift the sub up from the bottom. Austin met with the Venezuelan representative who is here to discuss the details."

"I'm ready. I don't think I could go another day like the past few days have been," Jack answered, feeling mellow from the meds, "I feel like I've just gone ten rounds with Iron Mike Tyson.

"That chump. Tyson never knew when to keep his mouth shut."

They fell into a comfortable silence, as only a couple of friends could do. Jack dozed, drifting in and out of drug induced nightmares. Strings of Chinese firecrackers were going off, blood red oceans were spinning him deeper and deeper, a woman's voice called to him but he couldn't understand what she was saying.

Jack sat up, popped another pain pill, and made the call he had been dreading.

"Aventura Memorial Hospital," a voice answered on the third ring.

Jack had forced all thoughts of Claire and any future they may have out of his mind, until he was finished with Burr.

"Yes. I would like to find out the status of Dr. Clair Marlow, please."

"Are you a member of the family, sir?"

"Sort of, I am engaged to her. We plan to marry when her divorce is final...." Jack knew he sounded like a blithering idiot.

"One moment, please."

"This is Nurse Adams, how may I help you?"

"My name is Jack Marsh. I am a close friend of Dr. Claire Marlow and need to find out her status, please."

"Mr. Marsh, Doctor Marlow was transferred to Madison Memorial in Wisconsin two days ago. Her husband, Dr. Marlow, made the request with the concurrence of the head of neurology here at the hospital. Mrs. Marlow has been placed in a long-term care facility. She is in a vegetative state and it is not known if or when she will recover. I suggest you contact Doctor Marlow yourself for more particulars. I'm sorry."

Jack was stunned. "Thanks," he said and tapped "end".

Jack refused to think about what he had just been told. He forced himself to think about eating, maybe a big thick juicy hamburger with thick slices of onion and mustard dripping out the sides…

'FUCK! FUCK! FUCK!' Why? It was his fault that Claire was shot …. his fault for getting her involved in his screwed up life. His mind was screaming for a drink to ease the pain and guilt. Just one drink to ease the pain, maybe a couple to help heal his self-loathing….

"Aaagh! I'm going fucking crazy! I am crazy. Oh God, what do I do now?"

"You suck it up, that's what you do." Tom said from the doorway. "Quit with the self-pity. You think you're the only guy that lost somebody they loved, or to have someone hurt that never recovered. Snap out of it Jack, you're not special. Claire's not feeling anything. To her, she's just sleeping. She either wakes up, or she doesn't and there's not a damned thing you can do about it. Tuck her away somewhere in your heart, and move on, Lad."

Jack stood, head bowed for a minute, pulling himself together, "I'm starving, you want to get a hamburger?

"The night was filled with stars overhead, the horizon a candle's breath of light. Jack was feeling a little stiff and sore, but overall not bad, all things considered. Some kind of ruckus was approaching the bungalow from the lobby. As the noise got louder, he recognized Mama Dey's voice castigating whoever it was with her.

"Talking to you is like talking to a coconut, I swear," Mama Dey said. "Jack, you up there somewhere, I can't see nothing, might even be snakes out here this time of night. Jack, can you hear me, boy?"

"Yes Ma'am, straight ahead, just follow the path," he said, as he started out to meet her and lead her back to the bungalow

"Tyrone, is that you?" Jack said to the giant shadow that blotched out the night.

"Sure is, Mr. Marsh, and Mama right behind me with a snake stick, prodding me every time I slow down."

Jack grabbed the big guy in a bear hug, "God, is it good to see you! You feeling ok?"

"I'm hungry. I ain't had nothing to eat in I don't know how long, except for some greens and cornbread out at Sister Oola's place this afternoon, but that wasn't nothing."

"Well come on up to the Bungalow, and we'll order you up a couple of steaks and pan fries."

"Don't go spoiling him. He's going back home to New Iberia and there ain't going to be no steaks on that menu, I can tell you for sure. They's as poor and skinny as yard chickens back there. They ain't got spit, much less rich folks food. Don't spoil the boy, Jack. He'll start getting all uppity and thinking he something special. Next thing, he'll be out preaching the word, and talking about things he don't even remember clear. Leave the boy be."

"A couple of steaks won't hurt him, Mama. How about you? You hungry?"

"Well, since you asked, get me one of them steaks too, but none of them pan fries. The grease gives me gas something awful."

An hour later, they were sitting around the table, full from the steak dinners, pie a la Mode, along with plenty of iced tea and coffee.

"Jack, my work is done here, I need to get on back to Key West. I'm worried about that Cloris girl. She's the one that had that baby right before we came down here to help out. I swear, if she got herself pregnant again I'm going to put a *jondecondelue* on that girl where she'll never look at a man again."

"Mama, I hate to see you go so soon. You should take a couple of days to relax, and enjoy the Island."

"*You* worse than coconut head here. *I* am going back to Key West and *you* is going to take me. You brung me here and now it's time to take me home. You think I'm going to conjure up a broomstick and ride it all the way to home? I know, lots of folks think I'm a witch, casting spells, stealing babies, and chickens and such, '*PISSHH.*' They don't understand nothin', they's not more than ten people like me around the world holding our old ways together. The scary part is this knucklehead next to you is one of them."

"Mama, why you talk bad about me all the time? Just because I got the *Shine*, don't mean you got to treat me like some New Orleans sissy boy. I done my share the last couple of days. I seen things ain't nobody seen before, and still be living…"

"That's enough, Tyrone. You've said enough. Ain't no need for regular folks to be knowing what's happening over across the line. You just shush up, boy."

"Shush up about what?" Bobbie said, as she came in and sat down at the table, checking the table for any leftovers.

"Hey Bobbie, how's Captain Price? Is he going to pull through?"

"Oh, yeah, he's already back to his old cantankerous self. He says he doesn't believe a word you say about how things went down on the *Sea Bird*. He said he knows you had to have a hand in killing Preston, just to shut him up."

"That's bull crap. Preston was that way when I found him. I'll admit to using his head as a bowling ball to throw Burr off, but I didn't touch the man below the neck, I swear."

"You know Price. He's just blowing off steam because he missed out on the action. He'll be flying back to Tallahassee tomorrow." Bobbie said as she picked at Mama's untouched pan fries and sopped them in cold steak juice.

"Girl, how come you never been married?" Mama Dey asked, taking Bobbie's hand in hers. "Good looking gal like you needs a family," Mama said, massaging Bobbie's hand and wrist. "I'm going to find you a fine young man to settle down with and raise some kids…"

"No way, Mama, don't put any hex on me. I'm perfectly happy being married to my job," Bobbie said, pulling her hand away from Mama's grip.

"All right, child, that the way you want it but if you change your mind you let Mama know."

"Mama, hold my hand," Jacob spoke up for the first time since polishing off a couple of pork chops and baked potato. "Is me and Kimmy going to …you know, how they say it back in Africa …. jump the stick?"

"Jump the stick? What you know about Africa, and courtship? You an Island Mon."

"Mama, you see this skin? What color is it? Of course I know about Africa. Who you think warned the world about the Blue Monkey on the loose? CNN?"

"Jack, where do you find these people?" Mama asked, shaking her head.

"Jacob, reach over here, and give me your hand," Tyrone said. "I'll tell you what you want to know."

Jacob reached out and clasped hands with Tyrone. His eyes grew huge, his body began to shake. Suddenly the two hands snapped apart like a small electrical spark. Jacob was ringing his hand, shaking it vigorously as if it were on fire.

"What you just do to me?" he demanded. "You trying to fry me?"

"I saw it all, Jacob, but maybe it's best if you don't know what it is I saw."

"I'm going to die, ain't I?" Jacob sobbed. "I got the Blue Monkey, ain't I?" he cried. "Tell me Mon, I can face it, is death coming for me tonight?" he blubbered "...Oh Lord, I'm too young, please don't make it tonight, Jack ain't paid me yet," Jacob prayed, eyes to heaven.

They all laughed at Jacob's antics.

"Give me your hand, Jack," Tyrone said.

"Uh uh, no way. I don't want to know anything about tomorrow or the next twenty years. That type of information is better left alone. Like Bob Marley sang, *Kay Sara Sara*."

"Bob never sang that song. He sang about a new day coming, but he was singing about the black mon, not the white mon," Jacob said, in the know.

"Forget all that foolishness. How am I getting home, Jack?" Mama asked.

"I'll go up to the front desk in a little bit and get everything set up for all of us. Tyrone, you're going to New Iberia, right, Mama to Key West, Tom and me to Louisiana?"

"Bobbie, you're going back with Captain Price, right?

"Yeah, he needs me around to yell at. Better watch out, Ace. You know he'll to want to see you face to face to get all the facts down at some point."

"That's fine; he can come down to the dive site. We'll be lifting gold up for the next couple of months."

"That ain't what I see, Jack," Tyrone said seriously.

"Shush, Boy." Mama Dey admonished. "He'll find out for himself soon enough."

End

Author's Note

In writing this novel, I was challenged to understand an area I had zero experience in, the world of Voodoo, and African Spiritualism. At first, I was overwhelmed with the amount of information available on the internet on both topics, but as I read and analyzed the data I started to see a common thread that runs back through millennia, and closely parallels the Jewish, Islamic and Christian beliefs, and ancient stories about God, and the beginning. The difference is the hundreds of small tribes and clans of Africa with their different languages and dialects relying on their Elders to pass down their beliefs through storytelling and rituals. An African Story Teller, for example, if asked to recite his tribe, or clan's spiritual history, will start out by saying. "In the beginning," the very same words that start the Old Testament. Their stories speak of a Garden where men were not allowed to go, they speak of the time when Giants walked the earth, the great flood, Prophets from the north, an end time. Rather than a heavenly destination of everlasting peace and love, the Tribes think in terms of good and bad spirits that can take many forms, and roam among them freely, to be worshiped and respected, feared and terrified of.

As the slave trade occurred, members of many different tribes were mixed together, each bringing their own belief system to the new world. As the horrors of slavery guided their lives, the different religions melded together, and became the glue the slaves used to see them through their misery. Spiritualism became very important to them, with each Plantation of slaves there was always someone that could interpret the events and signs around them. The Caribbean Islands, with Haiti having the harshest existence as slaves, became the home of modern day voodoo. Today, it is seen as a cult more than a religion, but even so, there are those that can see things beyond the normal, make things occur that would otherwise not be possible, manipulate a person's will, whether it be for good or evil, love or hate, pain or cure, it can be done, and with no reasonable explanation as to how.

Also, note that the Kakwa Tribe, Bakongo Tribe, and the Maa Tribe are real. Each as different as day and night, except in many common spiritual beliefs.

~MP, Key West

Made in the USA
San Bernardino, CA
18 July 2019